Books by T.A. Chase

Dracul's Revenge

Dracul's Blood
Anarchy in Blood

The Four Horsemen

Pestilence
War
Famine
Death
Peace

The Beasor Chronicles

Gypsies
Tramps

Home

No Going Home
Home of His Own
Wishing for a Home
Leaving Home
Home Sweet Home

International Men of Sports

A Sticky Wicket in Bollywood
Chasing the King of the Mountains
At First Touch
Blindsided
Burning Up the Ice

Serving Love at Carnival
A Grand Prix Romance
An Ace in the Tiebreak

Rags to Riches

Remove the Empty Spaces
Close the Distance
Following His Footsteps
Anywhere Tequila Flows
Walking in the Rain
Barefoot Dancing

Delarosa Secrets

Borderline
Snap Decision
Cold Truth

The Blood & Thorn Ranch

Bulls and Blood

Merging Violently

Fall into My Kiss

Every Shattered Dream

Every Shattered Dream: Part One
Every Shattered Dream: Part Two
Every Shattered Dream: Part Three
Every Shattered Dream: Part Four
Every Shattered Dream: Part Five

Sexy Snax

Two for One

Where the Devil Dances

What's His Passion?

Mountains to Climb
Climbing the Savage Mountain

Anthologies

Unconventional at Best
Unconventional in Atlanta
Semper Fidelis
An Unconventional Chicago
Unconventional in San Diego
Aim High

Single Titles

Out of Light into Darkness
The Haunting of St. Xavier
From Slavery to Freedom
The Vanguard
Ninja Cupcakes
Stealing Life
Lassoes and Lust
His Last Client
No Bravery
Always Ready
Possibilities
Ajay's Birthday Gift
The Unicorn Said Yes
Hearts on the Line

Fall into My Kiss

ISBN # 978-1-78651-347-2

©Copyright T.A. Chase 2016

Cover Art by Posh Gosh ©Copyright 2016

Interior text design by Claire Siemaszkiewicz

Pride Publishing

Published in 2016 by Pride Publishing, Newland House, The Point, Weaver Road, Lincoln, LN6 3QN, United Kingdom.

Pride Publishing is a subsidiary of Totally Entwined Group Limited.

Merging Violently

FALL INTO MY KISS

T.A. CHASE

Dedication

This is for everyone who has asked me about Edward.
He's finally getting his own story.

Chapter One

"Aren't you getting a little too old to be falling off your horse?"

Edward Monterrose glanced up from where he'd been staring out of the window. He grimaced when the strained muscles in his back protested the movement. "It was an unplanned dismount. Apparently Salt thought there was a shark in the liverpool jump and wasn't going to risk getting eaten by it. Yet he was willing to use me to distract the monster while he got away. Much like his father, Gypsy, did when he was competing."

His stepbrother chuckled and Edward smiled at the happy sound. Ever since Derek had fallen in love with Max Furlo and moved away from Nashville, joy had seeped into everything Derek did.

"I finally got a chance to listen to your latest album. I think it's your best yet," Edward commented as he pushed to his feet to greet Derek.

Derek pulled him into a gentle hug then kissed his cheek. "Thanks. Can't say I was happy to get a call from Scout saying you were in the hospital."

Edward shuffled to his bed and accepted Derek's help to climb back into it. "I'm sorry, but accidents are a hazard of the job. I was due to have a wreck at some point. It's been a while since I've lost my seat like that."

"You weren't expecting Salt to freak like that. He's been doing great since you both worked with Les." Derek pulled a chair up next to the bed then sat. He leaned back, crossing his legs while he studied Edward. "I guess I was imagining the worst, even though Scout said you were going to be fine."

"I won't be riding until the doctors clear me, which sucks. I'll have to withdraw from some of the big competitions and it'll hurt us in the year-end standings." He shrugged and winced.

Derek motioned to the cast and bandages. "What are your injuries? I didn't ask Scout, just chartered a plane to get out here as soon as I could. Left Max at the ranch to hold down the fort while I'm gone."

Edward snorted. "Hold down the fort? You make it sound like you're the one running the place. We all know Max is the reason why the cattle and horse part of your ranch is successful."

"You make it sound like I'm useless," Derek muttered as he pouted.

"You're useless when it comes to ranch work, brother. But you have other redeeming qualities. Your record label seems to be doing rather well." He shifted on the lumpy mattress, trying to find a spot that wouldn't cause his body to ache. Being covered with bruises made it difficult to get into a comfortable position.

"Are you going to tell me about your injuries?"

Wrinkling his nose, Edward sighed. "I broke three ribs and pretty much bruised every inch of my body on my left side from where I hit the ground. Also, I broke my left wrist and collarbone." He motioned to the sling keeping his arm tight to his chest.

Derek cringed in sympathy. "Thank God it wasn't worse, though you're going to be in pain for a while."

Edward nodded. "Yeah, but it's happened before. I'll be riding once I'm cleared."

"Even with a broken wrist and collarbone?" Derek sounded skeptical.

"I've done it before." Of course that was when he was younger and could rebound faster from an accident like this one, but he wasn't going to tell Derek that. "I have too much to do to let this hold me back for long."

Humming under his breath, Derek relaxed a little. "How's Salt doing?"

"He's doing fine. Didn't do anything, though Scout says he's acting a little embarrassed by the whole thing. As though he knows he did something wrong."

"Silly horse. He's been taking those jumps without a hint of trouble for months now. All of a sudden, he wigs out." Derek shook his head.

Edward laughed then groaned. "I need to remember amusement hurts."

A nurse walked in and smiled. "If you're in pain, Mr. Monterrose, I can give you something for it."

"No thanks. I can handle it." He leaned back against his pillows, letting her check his bandages. "Has the doctor said anything about when I can go home?"

"I believe he wants you to stay one more night, then he'll discharge you. Even though you were wearing your helmet, you did hit your head," she pointed out.

"Yeah. I know." He turned to look at Derek. "You didn't have to fly out here. I'm fine."

Derek waited until the nurse left before he replied, "You're the only member of my family I care about. When I hear you've been injured, I'm going to come and check on you myself. Now that I see you're doing as well as can be expected, I'll stay until tomorrow. Get you settled then I'll head back home."

Edward closed his eyes as exhaustion washed over him. He'd been walking around his room and the hallways since waking up that morning. Staying still and doing nothing had never been his style. If he wasn't riding one of his horses in a class or training session, he was working with his students and clients on their rides. It was rare for him to sit until after the horses were bedded down for the night.

"Your people will be helping out while you're healing, right?" Derek asked, and when Edward peered at him, he stared intensely.

"Of course they'll help. Not only my stable people, but

9

my clients and students will be taking care of things. Juan and Scout will take over working my other horses until I get cleared."

Derek smiled. "I guess no one will complain about you not riding when they have two other riders almost as talented as you to work their horses."

Edward shrugged. "I'm just lucky that Juan is only campaigning one horse this year or else he might not have been available to help me out. But it won't be long until I'm back in the saddle. I've ridden with a broken arm before."

"Which is completely idiotic," Derek commented. "You could do serious harm to yourself if you fell off again."

"I know that, Derek, but I'm not going to let this hold me back. Salt and I have a major show in Germany we have to ride in three months from now. I need to be ready and so does he. Unfortunately, no one else—aside from Les—can ride Salt the way he needs to be ridden." Edward rubbed the back of his neck and pursed his lips when a thought hit him. "Do you think Les would work with Salt for me while I'm grounded? I could fly Salt out there."

"Give him a call. I haven't talked to either Les or Randy for a couple days, so I don't know what kind of plans he has, though I'm pretty sure he won't say no to you."

"Can you get my phone out of the tray over there?" Edward motioned to where he'd left it by the window.

Derek retrieved it then tossed it on the bed. Edward picked it up, but didn't dial Les' number. He took a deep breath and tried to relax, yet all of his muscles were tightening up.

"I'll call him tomorrow. One more day won't matter, more or less," he muttered.

"How's the planning going for your charity event?" Derek inquired, willing to change the subject while Edward tried to get his thoughts together.

"Good. JoLynn and Katy have everything under control. You're still going to perform, right?" Edward shot him a worried look, knowing that part of the draw for the people coming was to get an 'intimate' performance by the

Grammy-winning country artist.

"Oh yeah. I told you…this is the kickoff for my upcoming tour." Derek checked his watch. "I should head out. Visitor hours are over. I'll be back in the morning."

Edward accepted Derek's hug. "Thanks for coming. Hopefully you'll be able to drive me to the hotel tomorrow at some point."

His brother patted him on his good shoulder. "Text me when you wake up."

"I will."

The room felt empty once Derek left. Edward picked up his phone to see whether he had any voicemails and saw that Les had called him. He looked at the clock, trying to decide if he should call his friend back that night or not. While he debated, his phone rang and Les' number appeared on the screen.

Taking a deep breath, he swiped his finger over it and answered, "Hey, Les."

"Edward." Les' voice still held a hint of his Southern drawl, though he'd been living in Wyoming for a couple of years now. "How are you doing?"

"I've had better days," he admitted.

Les chuckled. "I've been there and know exactly how you feel. How long will you be laid up?"

"The doctors say I should be grounded for a month or so while my ribs and collarbone heal." He trailed off while Les laughed again.

"So as soon as you get home, you'll be riding, huh?" Les understood Edward's thought process. "If I had been able to walk, I would've done the same thing."

Edward winced as he remembered how bad the injury that had ended Les' riding career had been. Les' mount, Whisky Sam, had slipped while taking off at a jump during a show. Les hadn't been ready for it and had fallen under Sam's hooves. The horse had done everything he could not to land directly on Les, but had still caught the side of Les' head with his hoof. Les had been in a coma for months then had had to learn how to walk and talk all over again.

It had been over a year before Les had climbed on Sam's back for a ride. Unfortunately, his career was over because he couldn't sustain another blow to his head. So Les had moved out to Wyoming and started raising cutting horses. There he'd fallen in love with a rodeo cowboy, finding a new life after feeling all he'd worked so hard for was gone.

Edward had taken his best horse, Gypsy, to Les for some additional training, bringing Les back to the show jumping world where he really belonged. It didn't matter that Les couldn't compete—he could still work his magic with the horses and their riders.

"Just don't tell Derek," Edward admonished Les. "I don't need to have him hovering over me."

"Of course I won't. How's Salt doing? He didn't get hurt, did he?"

Edward smiled. Just like Les to be concerned for the horse. "Scout said he's fine. Just embarrassed. I was actually going to call you tomorrow and see if I could send him to you for a refresher course. I swear he's like clockwork, every year or so, he needs to learn not to be scared of water jumps again."

"Like father, like son, huh? Let me check my schedule." Les hummed under his breath, and there was a rustle in the background that sounded like paper being shuffled. "Yes. Send him out whenever you want. I have a couple clients coming next week, but I can fit him in. Will you be coming out with him?"

"I wish, but I have a charity benefit to host, plus several students and clients I need to keep happy." He sighed, just the thought of everything he had to do making him tired. Being injured sucked all his energy. Usually he liked being busy every minute of the day. "One of my grooms will travel out there with him. When you think he's ready, I can come out and get him—or my groom can bring him back if I'm not up to riding yet."

Les cleared his throat. "He can stay as long as you need

him to. Will you keep campaigning him while you're out?"

Edward pursed his lips while he stared at the wall across from him. "I hadn't thought about it. I guess I'll talk to Juan and Scout. They're going to help out with schooling my young horses, so maybe Scout'll be willing to try Salt. Not sure though. He's a handful for me, and he likes me."

"You do seem to have the magic touch with him, but he does tolerate Scout and Randy. I'll have Randy ride him while he's here then Scout can take him when he's back. That should get you through the shows until you're able to compete." Les sounded as though he was thinking about how to organize the whole situation. "I could send my plane down to Florida to get the horse and groom. That way you don't have to haul him back to your place only to turn around and fly him out here."

"I'll ask Scout tomorrow when I get back to the hotel. They're only keeping me overnight. I'll probably head home the next day, but Scout still has a few more shows to ride in before he can head back to the farm. He can make sure Salt gets on the plane all right." Edward yawned.

A faint voice came over the line. He didn't catch what Les said in reply, but he did know it was Randy who was talking.

"Tell Randy I said hello," he told Les.

"I will. Now get some sleep and we'll talk in a day or two about the arrangements for Salt. Good night."

"Night, Les." Edward ended the call before setting his phone on the table next to the bed.

He climbed under the covers carefully after turning the overhead light off. Resting his head on the pillows behind him, he stared up at the ceiling. There were so many things he needed to make sure were taken care of by the time he got back home. Edward let his eyes drift shut. He'd worry about those tomorrow.

* * * *

"Are you sure you'll be okay? Do you have someone to travel with you back to Virginia or do you want me to hang around until you're ready to leave?" Derek helped Edward sit on the couch in his suite.

"I'll be fine. Scout will be back by noon and I'm going to go over to the showgrounds with him for the afternoon classes." He saw Derek's jaw tighten and he knew his brother was biting his tongue to keep from saying anything. "Don't worry. I'm going to rest until he gets here. I'm pretty sure most of my people there won't let me do anything more than walk from class to class. I need to be there to see how my students are doing, plus I want to check on Salt myself."

Derek sighed. "I shouldn't be surprised about this, but I wish you'd reconsider going there today. Why not take another day and rest? Then head out tomorrow with Scout."

Edward grimaced when his entire body protested as he shifted on the cushions. "I'll think about it and decide later. You might be right. It's hell getting old, brother."

"I agree. Of course, you're doing something that's slightly more dangerous than me." Derek set Edward's bag down next to the door of his bedroom. "I guess if you don't want me to stick around, I'll take off. I can catch a flight out of Orlando."

"Thank you for coming, even though you didn't have to." Edward accepted Derek's very gentle one-armed hug and kiss on the cheek. "I'm sorry you were worried."

Derek ruffled Edward's hair and chuckled. "I'll admit I always worry a little bit when you ride. I know you're very accomplished and your horses are some of the best in the world, but they're still animals and can be unpredictable."

"It comes from caring about someone. I worry about you too, though not nearly as much as I did before you met Max." Edward grinned at him. "So when are you two getting married?"

Rolling his eyes, Derek said, "Just because it's legal everywhere doesn't mean we need to run out and make our relationship 'official'. Besides, I think Tony and Brady are going to take the plunge first. At least that's what Tony said to Max last week when they visited."

Edward smiled, happy for them even as a rush of jealousy swept through him. He wanted to have the kind of relationship all his friends had, yet he seemed to be fated to wander the world alone.

Shaking his head, he tried to get over his pity party. He had a good life with great friends, family and a job he loved more than anything else in the world. There was someone out there for him — didn't matter if it was a man or a woman. He simply hadn't met that person yet.

"It'll be quite a gathering when it happens," Derek continued. "I'll call you when I get back to the ranch. And listen to your body, idiot. Don't go out to the show grounds if you're in pain."

"I promise I'll take it easy. Actually, before you go, can you help me to the bedroom? I think I'll lie down until Scout gets here."

After Derek left, Edward closed his eyes, trying to figure out the most comfortable spot on the mattress. He'd taken a pain pill earlier and knew it would drag him under eventually.

Chapter Two

Hunter tilted his head as he strummed the strings of his guitar then nodded—the notes were perfect. He started to play one of the original songs he'd written, but hadn't yet shared with the rest of the band. While he played, he glanced around the small park he sat in.

It was a pretty place, even in the fall, and just chilly enough that he had to wear a jacket over his sweater. The people walking by probably thought he was crazy to be out there, but after driving all over the Northeast with the guys, he needed some fresh air. Also, he needed not to be surrounded by people or walls.

Frowning, Hunter squinted, working a couple of the lyrics over in his head. He dug out a notebook from his backpack then wrote some words down. He'd organize his thoughts about that part of the song later. It was the melody driving him insane at the moment.

"You're rather good."

He jerked slightly when someone spoke beside him. He hadn't heard anyone approaching while he played. Turning, he looked up from where he sat and his eyes widened at the sight of the tall, dark-haired man standing close by.

"Umm...thanks," Hunter muttered as he glanced back down at his guitar. "It's something I've been working on."

"Do you mind if I sit?" The stranger gestured to the bench. "I'm Edward Monterrose, by the way."

Hunter shook Edward's hand before saying, "Hunter Lee. Sure, go ahead."

He watched as Edward eased onto the bench, catching the slight grimace he made when he bent. That was when he noticed Edward kept his left arm tight to his body and saw the end of a cast sticking out from the edge of the sling the man wore.

"You okay, man?" Hunter asked.

"Yes. I had an unauthorized dismount a couple of weeks ago. Broke some ribs, my collarbone and my wrist, plus bruised pretty much my entire left side." Edward shook his head. "You would think that at my age, I'd be prepared for my horse to freak out once in a while."

Hunter studied Edward then nodded. "You train horses?"

Edward grinned. "Is it that obvious? I train and ride show jumpers. My barn is about twenty minutes out of town." He pointed toward the western edge of the town.

"Cool. My band's toured some places in Kentucky and around here. I've always liked seeing the horses." He gave himself a mental shake. *I sound like an idiot. What is it about him that tangles my tongue? It's not like I haven't met good-looking guys before.*

Edward's smile brightened his dark eyes and Hunter blinked. He'd never seen a man's face look so open before. Usually the people Hunter dealt with always seemed to be hiding something from the world.

"The horses are the best thing about my job. I might be good at it, but I really do it because the horses are such amazing creatures." Edward shrugged. "Well, the horses and being able to travel all over the world."

Hunter chuckled. "That would be awesome. Maybe someday my band and I will be able to do that."

"Are you guys local?" Edward shifted slightly, grimacing and adjusting his sling.

"We're based in Arlington, but we travel all over as long as we can get a gig. The rest of the guys are home, since we just got done touring." He strummed his guitar once. "I wanted to unwind and I remembered this town from driving through. Thought it looked like a nice place to hang out for a little while before I head back."

Edward nodded. "Makes sense. You've been with them

for months. Need time away from them all. Doesn't matter how close you are. My brother's the same way."

Tilting his head, he studied the man sitting next to him. "Your brother's a musician?"

"Yes. Been doing music for most of his life. Did the whole big label thing then it burned him out. Now he's running his own label and happier than he's ever been." Edward's smile was soft.

"Cool. We'd like to be able to do that eventually. Just trying to get signed can be a bitch." Hunter sighed. "Can't help it, though. Music's always been the one thing I could count on. People come and go, but music stays forever."

Edward reached over to pat Hunter's shoulder. "I know what you're saying. Hey, do you happen to have a CD of your band I could have? I'd love to listen to it."

Hunter set his guitar aside then dug through his backpack to find one of the CDs he was never without. "Wouldn't be any kind of aspiring musician if I didn't have one, huh?"

"Thanks." Edward took it from him then glanced at his watch and sighed. "I have to go, but could I get your phone number? Maybe we could meet for lunch or dinner while you're still in town."

His odd combination of Asian and Hispanic ethnicities garnered a lot of interest from men and women—they tended to think of him as exotic until they got to know him, then they just thought he was weird. Surprise dashed through him at Edward's request. Edward didn't strike Hunter as the kind of guy who made a habit of picking people up in parks.

Even injured, Edward held an air of aristocracy about him. Hunter wouldn't have been shocked to find out he was from one of the wealthy families around Virginia. Of course, horses were expensive, so more often than not, only the rich could own more than one. Edward was definitely a member of the *one percent*—that much was evident just from hearing him talk and act. Hunter had run into a lot of the people turned on by his looks throughout his travels and had taken advantage of their fleeting interest in him, but there was something different about Edward.

"If not, that's fine too." Edward held up his hand. "I don't want to make you feel uncomfortable."

Hunter bit his bottom lip then shook his head. "Nah. It's good. Give me your number." He pulled his phone from his pocket and got it set up to input Edward's number. Once it was in there, he hit send and Edward's phone rang. "Now you have mine. I'll be around for a couple more weeks. Call me and I'd be happy to meet you."

Edward answered then ended the call before hopefully typing Hunter's name in his contacts. "I appreciate it. Now I need to get back to my farm. Have to make sure my employees aren't goofing off while I'm not around." He winked at Hunter before pushing to his feet.

Chuckling, Hunter nodded. "I get it. Take care."

"I will."

Hunter couldn't help but watch as Edward strolled way. He was a little disappointed that the coat Edward wore covered his ass. Hunter had no doubt Edward would have a premium butt. Shaking his head, he cleared his mind. No point in dwelling on it. If Edward called him, Hunter could find out. If not, he might have to man up and call the guy himself.

After playing a few more chords, Hunter couldn't get his mind back to the song, so he packed up his guitar then headed off toward the small café he'd discovered the day before. As he sat in a booth, his phone rang and he tugged it out of his coat pocket.

"Hey there, Lonnie," Hunter answered as the waitress approached him. He flashed her a smile of thanks as he flipped over his coffee mug and she filled it before setting a menu down in front of him.

"How's it hanging, man?" Lonnie sounded like he was smiling, which wouldn't have surprised Hunter.

Lonnie Balet, the lead singer of their band, had a cheerful personality. Helpful, considering how moody the rest of them could get as musicians.

"Low and to the left," Hunter answered as he doctored his drink.

Snorting, Lonnie said, "I really didn't need to know that."

"Then why did you ask?" Hunter laughed then continued, "What are you up to? You're not bored already?"

"Not necessarily bored. Just can't stand hanging out with my parents, you know. I mean, seriously, I think I was adopted or something," Lonnie whined.

"Hang on," Hunter told him when the waitress returned. "I'll take the hamburger and fries. Oh, and a piece of your cherry pie."

"I'll put that in." She took the menu before bustling off.

He put the phone back to his ear. "All right. What happened this time?"

His friend sighed. "It's the same old same old. Why don't I get a real job? I'm wasting my life with this stupid music obsession. Blah. Blah."

As much as Hunter wanted to be alone for a while, he couldn't let Lonnie deal with that shit on his own. "Do you want me to come home?"

"No, but I thought I might come hang out with you, wherever you are." Lonnie's hopeful tone caught Hunter's attention.

Huffing in mock annoyance, Hunter replied, "I guess you could come here. I got a room at a little B&B just outside of town. You could probably get a room there, or if not, you can stay with me."

"Thanks, man. I know you'd rather spend time by yourself, but I'm going crazy here." Lonnie grunted. "I can leave tomorrow morning. Shouldn't take me more than a couple of hours to get there."

"I'll send you the address to the B&B. Also, the phone number and you can call for a reservation." He grinned as his food arrived. "We can do some work on the next album."

"Cool. I'll call you in the morning when I head out." There was a voice in the background and Lonnie cleared his throat. "Have to go. Take it easy and I'll see you tomorrow."

"You too, buddy."

After hanging up, he tossed his phone on the table then started on his burger. God, at times there was nothing better than a burned piece of meat on a bun. The fries were hot and greasy as well. Perfect.

He hummed while he ate and the melody he'd been working on slowly sorted itself out. As he finished his fries, he wrote the music down in his notebook. *I'll play this for Lonnie when he gets here. Might work for the next album.*

Hunter finished his third cup of coffee and jotted down some lyrics to try with the melody. His waitress had dropped off the bill earlier. A young man entered the café, catching Hunter's attention. He was dressed in tight pants with knee-high boots that shined. The dark shirt he wore hugged his chest, showing off his flat stomach.

"Hey, Scout, you and Edward get back from Florida all right?" Hunter's waitress asked.

"Sort of, Rose." Scout grinned. "Unfortunately, Edward had a riding accident and was injured. Broken arm, collarbone and three ribs."

Ears perking up when he heard the mention of Edward's name, Hunter pushed to his feet before wandering over to where Scout chatted with the lady. He flashed Scout a smile when the man looked at him and held up his bill, but didn't interrupt.

"Oh no! He's getting too old for that." Rose shook her head. "Poor dear. I'll send you back with a piece of pie for him. Tell him to stop in the next time he comes to town."

"I will. I'm surprised he didn't do so today. He came into town earlier to talk to the mayor about the benefit we're having at the stables in a couple weeks." Scout shrugged.

Rose tsked. "Probably just busy. So many things he has to do. It's good that you and Juan are there to help him out."

Scout quirked one of his eyebrows. "You know better, Rose. Edward's going to be training riders when he's ninety. We're just all here to work for him."

Hunter studied Scout. The man's clothes were well-made and Hunter had no doubt the boots were hand-tooled. Everything about Scout spoke of money, just like Edward. Scout caught him looking and winked.

"Something tells me you don't work for anyone," Hunter murmured.

Rose giggled and Scout tilted his head to one side as he lifted his shoulder.

"You could be right, my friend. Mucking out stalls and hauling horse shit isn't my idea of a good day's work." He glanced over at Rose. "Excuse my French, Rose."

She flapped her hand at him. "I've heard that word before, Scout. I'm not innocent. You're a spoiled brat. Good thing Edward doesn't let you get away with anything. Here's your food."

Scout took the bag then leaned forward to brush a kiss over Rose's cheek. "Thanks, darling. I'll tell Edward you asked about him."

"Drive safe, honey." Rose turned to Hunter after Scout left, holding out her hand for the check. "You ready to check out?"

"Yes, ma'am." Hunter motioned in Scout's direction. "He live around here?"

Rose rang up Hunter's bill. "He's out at the Monterrose Training Center. Edward trains horses and riders— jumping, eventing and dressage. His family's lived around these parts for a hundred years or so. Founding family. Scout's not from Virginia. He's from New York, but he spends most of his time down here. He's a good guy, as is Edward."

Hunter loved gossipy ladies, not that he usually encouraged them. Rose seemed like a good sort and he couldn't help but feel curious about Edward. He opened his mouth to ask another question, but Rose handed him his change.

"Here you go. Come back soon." She nodded then shuffled off to wait on someone else.

After stuffing his change in his pocket, Hunter grabbed his guitar and slung it over his shoulder before walking out of the café. He glanced around the square that surrounded the park. There were others wandering around, but Hunter decided to head back to his room. Touring in a van with four other guys over thousands of miles could wear a guy out.

He'd slept pretty much the entire first two days he'd arrived at the B&B, leaving his bed only to grab something to eat in town then going back to his room. That day he'd actually gone for a walk to the park, yet he was still tired. Taking a nice, long nap before dinner sounded like a great idea.

Heading toward the edge of town, Hunter began humming the melody to his new song. It wouldn't let him go until he got it right. Heck, he'd probably dream about it while he slept. When that happened, he usually woke up with the complete melody in his head.

As he walked, he got his phone out to send quick texts to the other band members. They'd all scattered when they got back home. Andey and Scott had gone to visit their families and Boris had disappeared into New York City—none of them knew where he went on their breaks.

Hunter didn't think whatever Boris got up to was particularly healthy since the man always came back looking used up and bruised—and even more exhausted than when he left. Hunter could never bring himself to ask what his friend had done. While they were friends, Boris kept secrets from the rest of the band. Hunter knew that, but he was afraid Boris was going to end up dead at some point and that worried Hunter.

Scott and Andey replied almost instantly, complaining about their families, which was par for the course, even though they missed them while they were on the road. They could forget how confining being back home could be.

He was in his room and sliding under the covers when

Boris' text arrived.

Fine. See you in a week or two.

Short and sweet. Boris never had much to say. It didn't matter. He was a damn good keyboardist, so he didn't need to talk. Lonnie talked enough for all of them.

Good.

He texted back then tossed the phone on the nightstand next to the bed. Yawning, he stretched and settled under the blankets. Hunter curled around his pillow and closed his eyes. He needed to get his rest because once Lonnie got there, it wasn't going to be quiet anymore.

Chapter Three

"What are you listening to?" Scout asked as he entered Edward's office in the barn.

Edward glanced up from the computer screen and blinked, trying to focus on what Scout had asked. He'd been looking at numbers all morning, causing his head to ache. Rubbing his temples, he stared at Scout.

"What did you say?"

Scout flopped into the chair facing Edward's desk. "I wanted to know what you were listening to. It's good, or what I've heard of it."

After pushing away from his desk, Edward leaned his head back and closed his eyes. "I met this guy at the park in town yesterday. He was playing a guitar. We chatted a little bit and I asked him if he had a CD of the band he plays with. I like encouraging new bands."

Silence greeted his comment and he opened his eyes to see Scout staring at him. Closing his eyes again, he inquired, "What?"

"You should be wearing your glasses, especially after suffering a concussion." Scout pointed with his chin toward the steel-framed pair lying on top of some files. "If you put them on now, I won't tell on you when Lisa gets here."

"You're such a little snitch," Edward groused, but did as Scout said. He slipped them on then looked back at his friend. "Are you happy?"

Scout nodded. "Yes, I am. Now about this guy you chatted up at the park? I think I might have seen him at the café. Weird combination of Asian and Hispanic features. Nice thick, shiny black hair. Almond-shaped black eyes and gorgeous, high cheekbones. Tanned skin."

Edward frowned. "Weird? Why would you say that? Besides, from the way you're describing him, you obviously find him attractive."

"Just not a combination you see around here, especially the Asian part. And oh hell yeah, he's hot. Did you get his name and number?" Scout leered at him. "If he's just passing through, maybe you could hook up for the night."

"His name is Hunter. I got his number because I thought we could have lunch sometime." Edward shook his head. "And I'm not hooking up with him."

Scout huffed. "Dude, you haven't been laid in months. Not since you dropped that idiotic blonde bombshell, who unfortunately is the reason why there are dumb blonde jokes."

"She wasn't that bad, Scout. You didn't like her because she looks better in Gucci than you ever could." He grinned at Scout's disgusted sniff. "Why all of this concern about my sex life? It's not like I haven't gone months without sex before."

"True, but not while you're laid up. You need to find other things to occupy you until you're cleared to ride. Riding someone instead of a horse is a lot less stress on broken bones." Scout winked.

Edward covered his ear with his good hand, silently cursing the sling that kept his other hand strapped to his chest. "Christ! Scout, I don't want to hear that crap from you. You're like my little brother—or the son I never got around to having. You shouldn't be butting in to my love life."

Snickering, Scout clapped his hands. "You said butt."

"Oh my God, now you're like twelve years old. Get the hell out of my office and don't say another word about me getting laid." He pointed toward the door.

After jumping to his feet, Scout strolled out, waving as he disappeared. Edward sighed in relief then groaned when Juan walked in. Reaching over, Edward turned the music off.

"What do you want?"

Juan lifted his eyebrows at Edward's exasperated tone. "I saw Scout leave. Was he annoying you?"

"When doesn't he?" Edward shook his head. "Sorry about snapping. Thanks for coming in."

"I would've come in sooner, but I had a couple of horses to try out. I'm thinking about picking another up to show this year." Juan sat in the same chair Scout had just deserted, only he sat with a straight back, instead of slouching like Scout had.

"Find any that interested you?" Edward stood then paced around the office. He'd been sitting all morning and his bruised body had stiffened.

"Two. I had them put in the barn with Jekyll for now. If that's all right?" He eyed Edward.

Edward nodded. "Of course. There are empty stalls there. If there weren't, there are a few in the blue barn."

Juan smiled. "Thanks. Scout said you needed to talk to me?"

"Yes. Until I'm cleared by the doctors to ride, I need someone to take over my horses in the two shows I have coming up next month." He held up his hand to keep Juan from speaking. "Salt went to Les' for retraining. He freaked at the liverpool jump again. I wasn't expecting it, which is why I fell off. Even if he wasn't, I wouldn't have asked you to ride him. He responds best to Scout and Randy. He'll be back in a day or two. If I'm not ready to compete, I'll have Scout ride him in his next show."

Relief danced across Juan's face and Edward chuckled. He knew Juan and Salt didn't get along. There was just something about their personalities that made them butt heads. Sometimes horses developed idiosyncrasies and hating Juan seemed to be Salt's, along with fearing liverpool jumps. Their weird animosity entertained Edward.

"Scout is looking forward to that, I'm sure."

"Oh, he doesn't know." Edward winked at Juan. "But if

he wants to keep riding my horses, he'll do as he's told."

Juan shook his head. "You know threats don't work with him."

Edward huffed. "His parents should've beaten him more when he was young."

"True." Juan stood. "Are you going out to check over the horses? Your first student of the day should be arriving soon. I'll walk with you."

After stepping outside his office, Edward locked it behind them then strolled off down the hall to the front door. His office was in the main building which also held meeting areas and rooms where people could watching videos of their riding lessons. Also, there was a small cafeteria where his employees could have lunch or dinner if they didn't want to go into town to eat.

"How are the plans for the benefit going? I saw JoLynn and Katy walking around earlier." Juan held open the door for Edward. They paused on the front porch and glanced at the sprawling training facility before them. "Do you sometimes pinch yourself that all of this is yours?"

Edward slung his arm over Juan's shoulder. "I do, but then I look at all the paperwork that comes with this place, and I sometimes wish I wasn't in charge of it."

Laughing, Juan poked him gently in his side. "I bet you do miss those days when all you had to worry about was getting your two horses to different shows throughout the year."

"Now I have to figure out the logistics of getting fifty different horses to ten different shows during two months. Thank God I'm not in charge of riding them all." He sighed. "But I am in charge of getting their riders to those shows as well."

They climbed down the steps with Juan holding Edward's elbow to help balance him. Grimacing slightly, Edward pointed in the direction of the indoor arena before asking, "Aren't you interested in setting up your own training facility?"

Juan shrugged. "Yancey and I have talked about it, but at the moment, I'm happy working here with you. I have my own students and horses without having to deal with all the other shit that comes from owning my own place."

"It isn't as though Les wouldn't set you up with the perfect accountant and other people you need to be successful," Edward reminded Juan.

"I know, but I'm not interested in that right now. So about your benefit?"

"Right." Edward scrubbed his hand through his hair. "I guess planning is going well. The ladies don't really tell me anything unless they need me to sign for something—or pay bills."

He knew he was the financial backing for the benefit and he was fine with that. He believed in the charities they were going to be raising money for, so it didn't bother him to foot the bill.

"You and Yancey will be coming, right?"

"That's an idiotic question. Of course we'll be there. It's a chance for our family to be together in one place for the first time since Christmas. We've all been so busy no one's been able to meet up." Juan's smile was bright.

Edward tilted his head as he thought about the group of men and women he called his family. It included Juan and Yancey, Juan's husband. Randy and Les. Brody and Tony, Juan's uncle. Randy's sister, her husband and their children. They were all coming along with Derek, Max, Peter and Chaz, Peter's husband.

It was going to be a reunion, and Edward couldn't wait. After being alone with only Derek as family, to have so many people consider him a member of their family was almost like an embarrassment of riches.

"Oh, did you notice the music I was listening to when you walked in?" he asked as they entered the stables attached to the indoor arena.

"Yes. The band sounds good. Kind of alternative rock, right?" Juan motioned to one of the girls whose horse stood quietly in the cross ties. "Alicia, make sure you clean out her hooves. Don't want to have her get a stone bruise or worse."

Alicia scurried to do as Juan said. Edward hid his smile. A lot of the students who took lessons at Edward's training center worshiped Juan. Not that Edward blamed them—Juan was a brilliant rider who could guide any horse around a Grand Prix level show course and win. Almost any. Salt was one of the few exceptions.

"I guess. I'm not really up on genres or anything like that. I just know what I like. I was thinking about asking them to play at the benefit. Derek will be singing as well, but he's not going to do that all night." Edward edged out of the way as another girl led her mount into the arena. "I met one of the band members in the park yesterday. He gave me their CD. It'll be a paying gig. I wouldn't expect an aspiring band to play for free."

"But you expect Derek to do so?" Juan teased.

Edward eyed the two horse and rider combinations in the middle of the arena waiting for him. "Yes, because he's already made it. Even coming out didn't affect his career all that much. Actually ended up getting him a bigger audience. Giving his time to a good cause helps his image."

"True," Juan agreed before strolling ahead to check the girths for both girls. "Remember to double check them after you bring your horses in here. I know that your gelding has a habit of sucking in air to puff out his stomach. If you don't check, you'll wind up on your butt when you try to mount."

"Sorry, Mr. Romanos," the girl chirped. "I won't forget."

She'd forget again until she did end up on her ass. Some things people had to learn by letting it happen. A wet nose bumped Edward's hand and he looked down to see his dogs, Lilith and Basel, standing there. He crouched down to rub their ears while he waited for Juan to finish tightening the horses' girths.

Once Juan was done, Edward gestured for the dogs to

leave the arena and they followed Juan out. He knew they'd hang around, watching him. They were well-behaved, never barking or chasing the horses. They had kept him company since he'd moved into the small farmhouse a mile from the training center.

When he'd retired his stallion, Gypsy's Salt Mine, Edward had decided to buy an adjoining farm to start his own stud. Gypsy was his foundation stallion. The horse Edward had fallen off, Salt, was one of Gypsy's offspring. Highland Farms was Edward's real love. If he ever got too old — or too tired — of training horses and students, he would happily retire to the farm and breed horses.

"All right, Alicia and Tabitha. Let's walk your mounts around the arena. Remember, loose rein and keep them to the outside." He moved to the middle, so he could follow as they rode.

Two of his assistants had already set up four ground poles for the girls to take their horses over. Both were just beginning to consider jumping and they weren't ready for anything higher. In a couple of weeks, he'd raise the poles up to give them a bit of a challenge.

The lesson went well. The horses were old hands at the whole learning process, which was why Edward chose to use them with novice riders. There was nothing worse than high-strung horses freaking out young riders.

"Great job, ladies. Dismount and go brush them out. Remember to clean their hooves again. After you return them to their paddock, make sure their tack is cleaned and put back."

Edward was a firm believer in riders learning how to do everything. He taught them the proper way to groom and tack their horses before they even got on the animals. Having a groom do it for a rider wasn't right, in his opinion. A true horseman knew everything there was to know about their horse, and how to do every little thing as well.

He'd met his fair share of spoiled kids who'd always got whatever they wanted without working for it. If one of those kind showed up in his barn, they learned quickly that things were different with him. If a rider refused to tack up their own mount, he would refuse to train them. Riding was more than showing up and getting on a horse's back. Luckily, enough people realized that for him to have a full training schedule.

Once the horses were in the crossties, Edward headed toward the outdoor arena. He spotted two of his other assistant trainers as they strolled from one of the other barns.

"Melaney, can you and Spencer set up some three-foot jumps in the outdoor arena for me?" he called before they passed out of sight.

"Yes, sir." Melaney took a hold of Spencer's arm, pulling him behind her as she sprinted to the arena.

He grinned. Melaney's enthusiasm was one of the things he loved about her, and all the employees who worked for him at the training center and his stud farm. They truly found joy in being with the animals day in and day out. It was that happiness and a need to be with the horses that he looked for when he hired new people. He didn't want anyone there who was just doing it for the money.

Shit, there wasn't a lot of money to be made in the horse business. Coming from old money like Edward had was really the only reason he could keep doing what he loved, though he knew he'd have worked his ass off as a groom, mucking out stalls, all for a chance to ride—if he'd had to.

Chapter Four

Two days later

Hunter stopped playing when his phone buzzed. Lonnie glanced up from where he sat on the bed in their room. Hunter plucked his phone off the table next to him and checked the name. *Edward* showed up on the screen, causing Hunter to smile.

"Answer it already, instead of mooning at it," Lonnie groused.

Flipping his friend the finger, Hunter brought the phone to his ear. "Hey there, Edward."

"Hello, Hunter. How are you?" Edward's voice washed over Hunter like the finest silk sliding over his skin.

Hunter shivered. "I'm hanging in there."

Edward chuckled. "That's good. I was wondering if you would be interested in having lunch with me today. I'm coming into town for a business meeting."

"Umm…I'd love to, but a friend of mine is here," Hunter hedged, glancing over at Lonnie.

"Who's that?" Lonnie mouthed and Hunter shook his head.

There was a second of silence, then Edward said, "As much as I'd be happier to have you all to myself, I wouldn't be too upset if your friend would like to join us. Is he a member of your band?"

Hunter relaxed. "Yeah. He's our lead singer."

"Great. I actually wanted to talk to you about something, so having him here is fortuitous."

He frowned, trying to work out what Edward meant by

that word. "Huh?"

Edward cleared his throat. "Sorry. My brother says that I can be a pompous ass at times. Comes from my boarding school upbringing. Anyway, I just meant I have something to ask you about your band, and having another band member to chat with is good."

"Oh, okay." Hunter batted away the crumpled piece of paper Lonnie tossed at him. "When did you want to meet?"

"Around twelve-thirty at the café? I should be done with my meeting by then. If it happens to run over, I'll text you."

After pushing to his feet, Hunter set his guitar down then began to pace. "Sounds good to me. See you at the café."

"I'm looking forward to it." Edward hung up.

Hunter wandered over to the bed before flopping onto it, face buried in the pillows. "What the fuck just happened?"

"Sounds to me like you just made a date," Lonnie replied as he lay next to Hunter. "Who's Edward?"

"Just some guy I met in the park the other day," Hunter murmured.

Lonnie slapped his ass. "Just some guy? You don't act weird over just some guy. Tell me."

Rolling over, Hunter stared at the ceiling. "He's some kind of bigwig in the area. Trains horses at a place just outside of town. Talks and acts like he's got money."

"If he has horses, he has money. Can't afford the first without the second." Lonnie smoothed his hand over Hunter's stomach. The touch meant nothing, it was just something Lonnie did when he was thinking. "If he's just some guy, what's wigging you out about him? Does he scare you? Maybe he threatens you somehow?"

Hunter shrugged as he covered Lonnie's hand. "I don't feel threatened in a bad way."

Lonnie turned his head to look at Hunter. "Is there a good way?"

Snorting, he waved his hand slightly. "I meant I don't think he'll hurt me or anything. Just I get nervous around Edward. When you meet him, you'll understand. He's drop-dead gorgeous, Lonnie. He's older than us."

"Older?" Lonnie sounded horrified.

"Not like in his eighties or anything like that. He's maybe in his forties or so. I'm not good at judging age." He didn't care. Being in his early thirties, he could be considered old by teenagers. "Edward has a presence about him."

Lonnie eyed him. "Uh-huh. We run into gorgeous men all the time during our tours. What makes him different?"

"I don't know." Hunter rubbed his jaw. "And it's not like we spent a lot of time together or anything." He huffed in annoyance then pushed off the bed to pace around the room. "This is stupid. There's nothing special about him."

His friend studied him for a second then gestured toward the bathroom. "Why don't you go and clean up? We'll take a walk around town then sit in the park. I want to work the new song. Maybe we can get the lyrics right and send them to the others. See what they think. Well, not Boris. He won't do anything while he's in New York."

"Have you talked to him since he left?" he asked as he dug out a clean pair of jeans and a Henley from his bag.

"Nope. Got a short text the other day, letting me know he got there. How about you?" Lonnie picked up Hunter's guitar then set it against the chair.

Hunter grimaced. "Like you. A short text the other day, but nothing since. Why don't you send him another one? I hate that he goes there on his own."

"And looks like shit when he gets back," Lonnie commented, picking up his phone from the dresser. "Go get cleaned up. I'm going to head downstairs and wait for you while I check in with my mom." Lonnie rolled his eyes.

"Sounds good."

He shut the door behind him before dropping his clothes on the counter. Hunter turned on the water, letting it warm up while he undressed. Propping his hands on the edge of the sink, he stared at his reflection in the mirror and tried to figure out why the thought of seeing Edward got his nerves going. There honestly wasn't any reason why he should be worried about it. *Christ! It's like I'm a teenager again, getting a chance to see my crush. This is crazy.*

After testing the water, he climbed into the shower to wash up as fast as he could. He looked down at his cock, standing straight from his groin. Apparently the idea of talking to Edward excited him. He poured a little bit of conditioner into his hand then began stroking his shaft. Tightening his grip, he pumped faster and harder, knowing just how he liked his cock worked.

Hunter braced his other hand against the wall and let his chin drop to his chest. "Fuck," he groaned as he climaxed, spilling his cum onto the shower floor. He massaged his length until his touch made his skin ache. Once he caught his breath, he soaped up then rinsed off before he stepped out onto the bath mat.

He toweled off then dressed. When he was done, he went back into his room and put on his socks and shoes before he gathered all his other stuff to leave. Hunter headed downstairs and found Lonnie waiting for him. After slinging his guitar case over his shoulder, Hunter motioned to the door.

"Let's go." Hunter nodded at Sarah, the owner of the B&B, walking up from the kitchen at the back. "We're going to wander around town then hang out in the park."

"It's a nice day for a stroll. Will you be back in time for lunch?" Sarah asked.

"We're meeting someone at the café." He paused then continued, "Actually, we're meeting Edward Monterrose."

Sarah smiled. "Edward's a nice guy. He's having a benefit in a couple of weeks to raise money for some horse charity. Always invites the entire town, which we appreciate. We rarely get to rub elbows with celebrities and he has some famous friends."

Lonnie elbowed Hunter. "Are you ready?"

"Yes," he answered.

"Tell Edward I said hello and that I'm looking forward to the concert next month." Sarah waved them on their way.

"I will," Hunter told her as they left.

Since the B&B wasn't that far out of town and the roads weren't very busy at that time of day, Hunter and Lonnie decided to walk.

"Don't bitch about your feet hurting," Hunter warned his friend after Lonnie agreed to the stroll.

Lonnie rolled his eyes at him. "I'm not lazy. Besides, it's good to get fresh air once in a while. I should've brought my running shoes."

Hunter chuckled. "They do have shops here. I'm sure we could pick some up for you."

"Yeah. Let's do that. I like being able to run and it looks like there's not a lot of traffic most of the time around here." Lonnie studied the different shops as they wandered into town. "This one has possibilities."

Accepting Lonnie's backpack, Hunter said, "I'm going to the coffee shop two doors down. I'll grab you something to drink while you buy your shoes."

"Thanks."

He watched Lonnie enter the shop before moving down the sidewalk to the coffee shop. The young man behind the counter looked up and smiled.

"Hey, you're becoming a regular." Tad tossed the rag he'd been using to wipe the counter back toward the sink. "What can I get you?"

"Well, I can't go without my coffee in the morning," Hunter joked. While pulling out his wallet, he took a quick look at the menu, making sure he could get something Lonnie would like. "I need a venti caramel latte, two pumps with whipped cream and caramel drizzle."

Tad blinked. "That's not what you usually drink. Or at least not what you've gotten before."

He shook his head. "No. My friend decided to join me for the rest of my vacation, so he'll be around. He's buying a pair of running shoes next door."

"Cool. Likes to exercise, huh?" Tad worked on Lonnie's drink while he chatted.

"It helps with his breath control." At Tad's quizzical glance, Hunter laughed. "We're in a band together and Lonnie's the lead singer. He figured out that running helps with his stamina and breathing. Turned him into a fanatic."

Tad nodded as he set Lonnie's drink in front of Hunter. "Makes sense. You don't run?"

"I do, and I remembered to bring my shoes. All right. I'd like a venti chai with soy milk. No whip."

"That's the drink I remember." Tad started his drink. "So you're in a band, huh? What do you play?"

"I'm the lead guitarist, plus I tend to write most of our songs. We do a lot of original music, though we have a few covers in our set." Hunter heard the bell over the door ring and twisted to check that it was Lonnie. "Here." He shoved the latte at his friend.

Lonnie snatched it from him then took a sip. "M-m-m… thanks, man. Picked up some shoes. We'll go out later this afternoon."

"Here you go, Hunter." Tad eyed Lonnie. "This is your friend?"

He couldn't help but smile. Tad was checking Lonnie out and from the light in his friend's eyes, Lonnie was looking back. It seemed like he might not have to worry about entertaining Lonnie the rest of the time they were there.

Hunter wandered over to an empty table then set his drink down before getting his guitar out. There wasn't anyone else in the shop with them, so he settled in a chair and started to pluck at the strings. He checked his watch and saw he had an hour before he had to meet Edward.

Being friends meant he got to sit around while Lonnie flirted with Tad, which didn't bother Hunter too much. Lonnie'd been flirting with any man he found attractive for as many years as Hunter had known him so Hunter had gotten used to finding stuff to do while Lonnie hooked up. It gave him time to work out the last bit of melody that had been troubling him. After getting his journal out, he erased the old notes then jotted down the new ones.

He hummed softly then as the words came, he began to sing. Singing aloud was the only way he could make sure the lyrics worked with the music. Only after he finished did he notice there were people sitting and standing around, listening to him. Glancing back over to the counter, Hunter saw Lonnie leaning against it, arms crossed and with a bright smile on his face.

"Sounds pretty good, Hunter," Lonnie called. "Why don't you sing something else?"

Shaking his head, he gestured for Lonnie to join him. "If they want to hear another song, I think you need to sing it."

Lonnie gave Tad a questioning look and the barista nodded. "All right. Let's give them a little concert. We can do a couple songs before we have to be at the café."

"Bring me a glass of water," Hunter ordered.

"Yes, sir." Winking at him, Lonnie got a glass from Tad before coming over to sit next to Hunter. "Pick a song."

After taking a sip, Hunter bent over his guitar and played. Lonnie hummed a few bars then sang. Hunter loved listening to his best friend's voice. At points, it was bright and clear and at other moments, deep and gravelly. But always full of emotion.

Hunter didn't even pause, just went right into the second song, knowing Lonnie would follow his lead. The final notes of the third song faded and Hunter leaned back in his chair, flexing his hands.

The applause startled him as he stretched. More people had come into the coffee shop and Tad was busy filling their orders. Grinning, Lonnie stood then bowed. Hunter checked his watch and swore.

"Shit! I'm going to be late." He jumped to his feet.

Lonnie grabbed hold of his arm. "I'll put your guitar in its case and be along in a few. This way you don't make a bad impression by being late on your first date."

He thrust the instrument at his friend. "Make sure you show up at some point. Don't bother Tad too much, especially since it's gotten busy in here."

"Don't worry about me. I'll be there shortly. Besides, you should be happy to talk to the man without me hanging around, eavesdropping." Lonnie shot a quick look over at Tad, who flashed him a smile before waiting on the next person in line.

Hunter huffed. "Only you would arrive in a small town and pick up someone at the local coffee shop."

Lonnie punched him in the arm. "What's got your nose out of joint? Weren't you the one who picked up a guy in the park a couple days after you arrived here? So you can't yell at me for hooking up with Tad."

He couldn't argue about that. "Tad will give you directions to the café."

Not waiting for Lonnie to reply, Hunter dashed from the coffee shop and down the sidewalk toward the café. He spied Edward talking on his phone while walking from the opposite direction. They got to the café at the same time.

"I have to go, Derek. I'll call you tomorrow," Edward said to whoever he was talking to then ended the conversation. His expression seemed to say he was happy to see Hunter. "Talk about great timing, huh?"

"Yeah." Hunter took a deep breath, calming his racing heart.

Edward opened the door then motioned for Hunter to go in. "Did your friend decide not to come?"

"Oh, Lonnie will be here eventually. Probably after he gets Tad's phone number," Hunter told him.

"Tad at the coffee shop?" Edward didn't wait for Hunter to answer before he greeted Rose. "How's one of my favorite ladies?"

Rose hugged him. "Scout said you were injured at your last show. You need to take better care of yourself. You're not getting any younger, Edward."

Hunter bit his lip to keep from laughing at the sight of the tall man being scolded by the petite white-haired lady. "Can we sit anywhere, Rose?"

She pointed toward a booth a little farther in the back.

"You can sit there. Just the two of you?"

"I have a friend joining us at some point," Hunter told her as they wound their way through the café.

"All right. You boys want something to drink?" Rose set menus on the table.

"I'll have coffee," Edward said as he took a seat.

"Iced tea, please?" Hunter sat across from him then waited until she'd left before he answered Edward's earlier question. "Yes, that Tad. Lonnie forgot his running shoes at home, so he stopped at a shop to pick a pair up. I went to the coffee shop to get something for us to drink. We were just going to wander around the square then sit in the park, working on some songs. Lonnie took one look at Tad and I knew we weren't getting outside again until I had to meet you here."

Hunter wanted to slap himself upside the head. He was rambling, and he was pretty sure Edward didn't want to hear all that crap.

Edward thanked Rose when she dropped off their drinks, but told her they needed a few more minutes to decide on lunch. "Tad is quite good looking. I'm not surprised your friend would ask him out. What did you do while Lonnie and Tad were flirting?"

"Worked out the melody and the lyrics for our newest song. Then Lonnie and I had a little impromptu concert, which he was happy to do because it would impress Tad. Anything that gives him a chance at getting laid." Hunter shook his head. "Lonnie's a bit of a slut, though I think most musicians are at some point in their career."

"My brother was for sure. Then he fell in love and all his one-night stand days are behind him." Edward chuckled. "Are you — or were you — a slut?" There was a slight smirk on Edward's face.

Hunter's cheeks heated, but he admitted, "If I'm given the chance, then I usually take it, but I don't think I'm quite as bad as Lonnie."

"Well, that means there's a possibility for us then,"

Edward joked.

"I guess."

Rose approached their table just as Lonnie stepped into the café. Hunter waved to get his attention and Lonnie loped over to join them.

"Edward Monterrose, this is my friend Lonnie Balet. He's the lead singer of our band," Hunter introduced them.

"It's great to meet you, Edward." Lonnie shook Edward's good hand then flopped into the chair next to Hunter.

Chapter Five

Edward watched as Lonnie charmed Rose. Having heard Lonnie sing on the CD Hunter had given him and seeing Lonnie's charismatic personality, he understood why the man was the lead singer in Hunter's band.

Once they'd ordered and Lonnie was settled, Edward asked, "Why did you name your band Merging Violently?"

Hunter and Lonnie burst out laughing. He waited patiently until they were done, then he lifted his eyebrow in question. Hunter smiled.

"Let's just say none of us got along when we first met. A lot of clashes, but we figured out we made better friends then we did enemies. Then we realized we all played instruments and that Lonnie could sing, so we decided to start a band." Hunter poked Lonnie in the arm. "That was in high school. We've been together since then."

"Who all is in the band?" Edward found he wanted to know everything about Hunter, and the band was one way to do that.

"Hunter should've said that four of us went to school together. Andey, Scott, Hunter and I knew each other through much of school, though it wasn't until our senior year that we became friends," Lonnie explained. "Boris joined us on our third tour when we decided we needed a keyboardist. He's amazing. Could probably make a living as a concert pianist."

Hunter shook his head. "Boris has too many demons haunting him. I don't think he'd be able to deal with the pressure being one of those would put on him."

Edward frowned. "Is he from your home town? Or did

you find him somewhere else?"

"Boris found us in New York City. We were playing at a small club there and he approached us after the show. He was too good for us to pass up." Lonnie pursed his lips and paused for a second before he spoke again. "I still don't understand why he'd want to travel with us."

Rose brought their food and there was silence while they took their first few bites. Edward swallowed then cleared his throat.

"I'm putting on a benefit event at my training center and I was wondering if you would consider performing for it." He leaned back in his chair.

Hunter's blue eyes widened in surprise. "Are you kidding?"

Chuckling, Edward said, "No, I'm not. I listened to the CD you gave me, Hunter, and I think you're really good. My brother is going to perform, but he's doing a small set. I'd like your band to play throughout the night. I'll pay you."

"Sarah at the B&B told me to let you know she was looking forward to the benefit." Hunter smiled. "Who is your brother? I've heard about him and something tells me he might be a big deal, but I don't think I've ever heard his name."

"Derek St. Martin. He's technically my stepbrother, but we don't think of ourselves that way. He's the only one I really consider family." He shrugged.

Lonnie stared at him with his mouth half-open until Hunter nudged him. "Sorry. I'm not a big country music fan, but even I know that name. He's the guy who came out then left the record company to start his own."

Edward nodded. "Yes. His own label has been doing really well too. I'm proud of him. He was a complete mess until he met Max, his husband. Once they got together, Derek decided he couldn't live in the closet anymore. He took a slight hit when he first came out, but now things have settled and are going well for him."

"And he's going to be at your party?" Excitement made Lonnie's voice shake.

"Yes. He's agreed to launch his new tour with a private concert at my benefit." Edward grinned. "Derek usually hangs around at these events, so I'm sure he'll hear you."

Hunter turned to Lonnie. "We'll have to ask the others. Remember we don't do anything without making sure it's all right with the guys."

Lonnie nodded. "You're right. We'll call them tonight and tell them. Of course, we might not be able to get a hold of Boris."

"If he doesn't get back to us, we'll play without him. It wouldn't be the first time." Hunter caught Edward's gaze. "Like we've said, Boris has some issues."

Edward sighed as he leaned back to let Rose fill his coffee cup again. After she left, he said, "I've known many people like that. Not just in the music business with Derek, but in the horse world as well. Everyone deals with their problems in different ways. Some are more destructive than others."

"True." Lonnie motioned to Edward's arm. "What happened?"

"Fell off my horse."

Hunter snorted. "Something tells me that doesn't happen very often, considering you own a training center and all."

Grimacing, Edward fixed his coffee with a little sugar and creamer. He took a sip then replied, "That's true. I haven't fallen off my horse in maybe four years. I wasn't expecting Salt to balk at the liverpool jump."

"Salt? Liverpool jump?" Lonnie grinned. "What's that? Some weird kind of Beatles obstacle?"

"Salt is the stable name of my main ride. Gypsy's Salty Liar is the offspring of the best horse I ever had, Gypsy's Salt Mine. A liverpool is an open pool of water the horse must jump during the course of a round. It might be around ten feet across from takeoff to landing. There are jumps where water is underneath a set of rails, so a horse and rider have to clear the rails and the water. For some horses, it might

be a little more distracting than a wide open liverpool."
Edward paused when he saw the slightly glazed look in
Lonnie's eyes. "Sorry. It's my career and my passion."

Hunter reached out and touched Edward's hand. "Don't
worry. I get carried away when I talk about music. I find
your enthusiasm attractive."

His cheeks warmed and Edward ducked his head a little.
*Christ! How old am I? I've flirted with some of the best-looking
people in the world. Yet a guitarist from an unknown band makes
me blush like a teenager with his first crush.*

"And that's my sign to leave," Lonnie commented,
pushing back his empty plate then his chair. "Hunter, can
you cover me? I'll get the next one."

"Don't worry. I'll buy today since I asked, plus it was
kind of a business meeting." After standing, Edward held
out his hand. "It was nice meeting you and I hope you end
up deciding to play at my event."

"Thanks, man." Lonnie shook his hand firmly then
winked at Hunter. "I'll take your guitar along with my
shoes back to the B&B. Catch up with you later."

They watched Lonnie leave before Edward sat back
down. He chuckled. "I think you chased him away."

Hunter burst out laughing and it took a minute for him
to compose himself. Edward simply waited, though he
shifted in his seat because seeing the joy on Hunter's face
got him hard.

"Hell no. Lonnie left so we could be alone. There was no
chasing." Leaning over, Hunter took Edward's hand in his
then squeezed a little. "He knows I'm really interested in
you. To be honest, I'm impressed he bolted. Usually he'd
stick around to bug me."

Edward twisted his wrist a little, checking his watch.
"I'm thinking part of the reason he left is because Tad just
finished his shift. I bet they're either heading to Tad's or
to his room at the B&B." He quirked his eyebrows when
Hunter groaned. "What?"

"I hope he doesn't take him back to the B&B. We're sharing

a room since there weren't any left. Also, there's only one bed." Hunter huffed in annoyance. "Though I wouldn't be surprised if he did."

"Have you and Lonnie ever slept together?" He probably shouldn't have asked, but he couldn't help it.

Hunter wrinkled his nose. "Once, but it didn't turn out well. Probably the worst night of both our lives. Never did it again."

"You turned out better friends than lovers?" Edward had a few friends like that.

"Not really. We've always been friends and if things had gone well that night, we'd have stayed lovers. But it was awful." Hunter chuckled. "Ask Lonnie. He'll say the same thing. Thank God we never tried again."

Edward glanced up when Rose brought over the bill. "Thanks, Rose." He took out his credit card then handed it to her. "Would you like to go for a walk in the park? I don't have to be back to the center for another hour. Since I can't ride and my doctor has told me to take it easy for another week, I have friends working with my students as a special treat to them. My clients are all going over their regular training routines for a show this weekend."

After standing, Hunter held out his hand. "I'd love to go for a walk."

"Great." Edward went to the counter where he signed the credit card slip before taking his card back from Rose. "Have a good day, Rose."

"You too, Edward." She smiled at Hunter.

As they walked out of the café, Hunter tucked Edward's hand in the crook of his elbow. They strolled across the street to the park. Edward liked the idea of walking as part of a couple. He smiled at some of the familiar faces he remembered seeing around town.

"Do you mind walking like this?" Hunter waved his hand between them. "Are the people who live around here open-minded?"

He lifted one of his shoulders, wincing slightly when

a hint of pain danced through him. "Most of them are pretty much 'live and let live'. They don't really care, plus I'm respected here because I don't treat them like they're beneath me. I've seen quite a few of my clients do that to those who don't have the money they do."

"Scout didn't seem that way. At least, he was really nice to Rose yesterday," Hunter told him.

Snorting, Edward rolled his eyes. "It took a while for me to get Scout's head out of his ass. So arrogant and thought he was the greatest thing to happen to the world. I had to knock him down a few pegs along the way, but he figured it out and grew up."

Hunter wrapped his arm around Edward's shoulders, drawing him closer. Edward encircled Hunter's waist and sighed. It had been a long time since he'd had this kind of intimate contact with someone. Oh, he'd had sex, he hadn't been celibate, but he'd long ago learned there was a difference between sex and intimacy. It was nice.

"We all know people like that. Maturity turns them into actual humans." Hunter directed them toward a bench under a large oak tree, off the heavily trailed path.

"Obviously Lonnie hasn't grown up yet," Edward joked.

"No, he hasn't, but I'm not sure he ever will. He can be a complete ass at times, but for the most part, he's harmless. He treats everyone the same—famous or otherwise."

Edward sat, sighing as he tugged on the sling keeping his left arm near his body. Moving the strap eased some pressure on his neck. He smiled at Hunter who'd taken his hand.

"Do you think your friends will say yes to playing?"

Hunter pursed his lips as he seemed to be thinking, then he nodded. "Yes. It'll be an easy gig. We won't have to travel too far to do it, plus it'll give us a chance to play in front of Derek St. Martin. Everyone knows he's got an eye for talent, and not just country music either. Who's to say he won't decide to give us a chance after he hears us?"

I'll have to make sure to send Derek their CD before next

month. Edward made a mental note. He was always willing to help someone out. His father had done that for him when he was seventeen and wanted to ride horses for a living. It was the same crazy kind of dream that had Hunter and his bandmates traveling all over the country, doing gigs for the chance at a shot for a record deal. He wouldn't promise anything would come of Derek hearing the band, but he'd at least get them a chance to be heard.

"There'll be some high-powered people there. Also, ones in important positions throughout society. If Derek doesn't work out, someone else might know someone who can help you. While these benefits help raise a lot of money for charities, they are wonderful places to network. Get your name in front of people." Edward bumped their shoulders together. "You might even end up with more gigs out of it."

Hunter rested his back against the bench. "That'll be nice. Help get us seen by a different group of people. What is this event for?"

Edward let go of Hunter's hand to reach into his inner pocket. He pulled out a piece of paper then gave it to him. "I worked with several horse nonprofits. Mostly those that take thoroughbreds from off the track and retrain them for other disciplines."

"Other disciplines?" Hunter frowned. "What do you mean by off the track?"

"It means that these charities adopt—or are given— thoroughbreds that aren't being raced anymore. They might have been retired due to injuries, or because they just don't have the heart—or interest—in running. There are even a few who were never raced at all. They didn't have the talent for it." Edward gestured toward the pamphlet. "Instead of sending them to slaughterhouses or wherever, and if they aren't viable for breeding purposes, some trainers and owners give them to these charities."

Hunter tilted his head, reading the flyer. "I guess I never thought about what happens to them once their racing careers are over with."

Edward exhaled softly. "A lot of people don't, but we're doing our best to get the information out there. Also, retrain the ones who are healthy for new jobs. I take one or two every year and work with them. Some of them are natural jumpers. Others move so beautifully, they're perfect for dressage. Once they've been given some basic groundwork, I find them new owners."

"Wow, that's cool. What happens if they can't be used for anything? Like their injuries are so bad, that they can't take the punishment of riding, jumping and anything else? But aren't bad enough for them to be put down?" Hunter folded the paper before slipping it in his jacket pocket.

"Some of the charities allow them to be adopted as companion animals. The adoptee knows the horse isn't to be used as anything other than a paddock companion for another horse or for the adoptee themselves. Others are retired to wonderful farms that will keep them until they die of old age." Edward smiled. "Heck, at times I think they live better than I do."

Hunter studied him. "I'd love to come out and see your place."

Edward dug his phone out of his pocket and double-checked his schedule. "If you and Lonnie would like to come out tomorrow afternoon, I'm free from two until four. I can show you around. You can see the training center and my breeding farm."

"I'll be out for sure. Whether Lonnie comes will depend on if Tad has to work or not." Hunter took a quick peek at the time on Edward's phone. "I guess you should probably be heading back soon."

He did have to go, but not before he tasted Hunter. After cupping the back of Hunter's head, Edward angled his chin, bringing their lips together in a soft kiss. He wanted to make sure there was more than just a physical attraction between them. There needed to be a connection that went deeper than lust. Oh, not that he wouldn't have been more than happy to take Hunter to his bed, but at this point in

Edward's life, he found he was searching for something more than just sex.

Hunter allowed him to control the kiss, opening to him without protest and resting his hands at Edward's waist. Edward swept his tongue in, savoring the hint of coffee mingling with an underlying minty flavor as though Hunter had been chewing gum earlier. He eased closer to Hunter while doing his best to remain aware of approaching footsteps.

The town was rather easy-going about things, but most of the townsfolk didn't appreciate public displays of affection by any couple — straight or gay. It just wasn't done in polite society and Edward always did his best not to rock the boat. He'd rarely kissed any of his girlfriends in public, so it wasn't as though he were ashamed of the men he dated. Keeping his relationships private was important. After seeing how vicious the media could get when Derek had come out, Edward had decided it was best just to keep things under wraps.

Footsteps approached, so Edward ended the kiss, putting a couple of inches between him and Hunter. He stared into Hunter's dark eyes, seeing emotions swirling in them. What those were exactly, Edward couldn't tell, but he liked the idea that he might be causing a little turmoil. The man was certainly messing with Edward.

His phone buzzed at that moment and he looked at the screen. It was Juan. "I have to take this."

Hunter licked his lips and nodded. "Of course."

After pushing to his feet, Edward walked a few feet away before he answered. "Hey, Juan."

"Edward. I'm sorry to call. I know you said you'd be back by two, but I was wondering if you could come back earlier." Juan sounded rushed.

"Is everything okay?" Edward asked, already getting his keys out.

"Yancey got kicked by a cow and is on his way to the hospital. I need to go there, but I have a student coming in for a lesson." Juan growled under his breath before continuing, "She's new and I don't want to postpone it."

Edward motioned to Hunter. "I understand. I might not be able to ride yet, but I can help her from the ground. Leave me her information about where she's at and what you were going to do today, and I'll take care of it."

Juan sighed. "Thanks, Edward. I appreciate it."

"You've done a lot of covering for me since I was hurt. Consider it payback. It's not like I wouldn't be working with her at some point anyway. Get to the hospital safely and let me know if there's anything I can do for you and Yancey. Do you need someone to take care of your dogs?" Edward led the way out of the park.

"No. One of Yancey's vet techs is going to feed and walk them for us. If we end up having to stay at the hospital overnight, I'll call." Juan didn't sound overly worried about Yancey, but still it was scary anytime a loved one was injured. "I'm getting into my truck now. Talk to you when I know something more."

"All right." Edward ended the call then informed Hunter, "I have to head back to the center. One of the riders who gives lessons at my place has a family emergency, so he needs me to take over one of his students today."

Hunter nodded. "I caught the gist of it. As much as I'd love to continue our little make-out session, I understand. How about I text you tomorrow morning for directions to your place?"

He brushed a quick kiss over Hunter's mouth. "Sounds great to me. Thanks for understanding and I'll see you tomorrow." Edward waved then dashed off to his truck. He needed to get back to the barn and read Juan's notes before the student got there. He wanted to have a basic idea about her, so he could help her work on her riding.

Chapter Six

As disappointed as Hunter was about Edward having to cut their time short, he had enjoyed the kiss. He walked down the hall to his room and checked the door before he opened it. He didn't want to walk in on Lonnie and Tad doing anything.

There wasn't a towel or any of the other predetermined signs of having sex on the doorknob, so Hunter went in. Glancing around, he spotted his guitar leaning against the chair and the bag holding Lonnie's new shoes.

After stripping off his jacket and shoes, he flopped onto the bed with his phone. He brought up Lonnie's number so he could text him.

At the room. Edward had an emergency. Needed to get back to his place.

He dropped the phone on the blankets next to him, figuring it was going to take a few minutes for his friend to get back to him. Hunter stared at the ceiling and let his mind drift while he waited. Music danced through his brain like it did every time he had a minute of quiet.

Sighing, he rolled off the bed to crouch by his backpack and dug through it, searching for his notebook and pencil. Once he'd found them, he crawled back on the mattress, leaned against the pillows then opened his book. Another song began to appear on the paper as Hunter wrote. The lyrics would come later once he got the melody down. Also, Lonnie would help with the words.

He'd be the first to admit he was better at melodies than

lyrics. Most of the time Lonnie or Boris would write those. The music was his world, which fit in perfectly with the rest of the band.

His fingers twitched, so he picked up his guitar then started playing bits and pieces of the drifting melody. While he played, his phone buzzed and he paused to check it.

Sorry you didn't get lucky. Catch you for dinner.

Don't have too much fun. See you later.

He sent the text then let his phone fall to the floor. More music waltzed through his head and he started composing. Hunter had the feeling it was going to be a long day and night. In a way, it was good that Lonnie was busy with Tad, so Hunter could allow the muse to take over.

* * * *

The door swung open just as Hunter put the finishing touches on his third song. He dropped his pencil then stretched his arms over his head. Lonnie slipped into the room, freezing when he spotted Hunter on the floor.

"What are you doing down there?" Lonnie shut the door behind him before strolling across the room to drop onto the bed.

Hunter glanced at the clock on the nightstand and yawned. "You know how it is when the muse hits, man. I've been up since I texted you working on some new songs. You'll have to listen to the melodies and help with the lyrics, then we'll see if they're good enough to go on the next CD."

"Cool." Lonnie didn't move, but sighed.

After propping his guitar against the chair, Hunter pushed to his feet then climbed on the mattress to lie next to Lonnie. "Did you have a good time?" He paused for a second before continuing, "Well, obviously you must have had a good time since you're just getting in."

"It was great." Lonnie rolled over and rested his head on

Hunter's shoulder. "But I won't be seeing Tad again."

"Why not?" He couldn't help but ask, even though he'd heard that statement a hundred times before.

"He's young and not looking for anything serious." Lonnie punched him when he snorted. "Not that I am either. I'm just getting too old for one-night stands."

"You're not getting too old. You're just maturing and realizing that jumping from bed to bed isn't healthy or fun anymore. Being a musician makes it easy to find sexual partners. Of course, I know you, Lonnie. You're not going to stop this until you find the right person."

Lonnie pushed up on his elbow to look down at Hunter. "What about you? Is Edward the right person for you?"

He shrugged. "It's too soon to tell. We've only known each other for a couple of days and it's not like we've had a lot of time together."

"What about today? I thought I gave you plenty of time for something to happen." Lonnie eyed him.

"We kissed in the park." Hunter closed his eyes when Lonnie hooted in excitement. "Stop it, asshole. It didn't last that long. He got a call and had to leave."

Lonnie flopped back down then snuggled close. "That sucks. But how was the kiss? Nice?"

"It was fine." He didn't want to talk about it right then, so he chose to change the subject. "How cool is it that we're going to get a chance to play in front of Derek St. Martin? All the industry gossip says that his label is doing really well. He's signing some great artists."

Luckily, Lonnie was willing to go along with him. "It's a great opportunity, but don't get too carried away. We've been signed to a label before and nothing came of it."

He tapped Lonnie on the side of the head. "When did you become the voice of reason? Weren't you the one who convinced all of us that this could be our dream and we could succeed at it if we all just put in the work?"

"Ow!" Lonnie rubbed his head. "Maybe with age comes caution. I just don't want you — and the others — getting

55

your hopes up that St. Martin will fall in love with us. Sure, he's signed some alt and rock bands, but most of them are country. It makes sense since he's a country singer. Just try not to get your hopes up. I don't want any of you disappointed."

"Well, we have to talk to the others about it." Hunter looked around for his phone.

"Dude, the only one who might still be up is Boris, and I doubt he'd get back to you right away." Lonnie sighed and Hunter could almost hear the worry in his friend's voice. "I'll text Andey and Scott in the morning. You get Boris. He seems to respond better to you than me."

Hunter yawned then nodded. "Yeah. I can do that. Hey, Edward invited us out to his place tomorrow afternoon. You want to go?"

"Sure," Lonnie answered before he crawled off the bed. "I'm going to take a shower."

After Lonnie disappeared into the bathroom, Hunter put away his guitar and his notebook. He grabbed his phone from where he'd tossed it. When he looked at the screen, he grimaced. There was a text from Edward. He must have missed the buzz while playing.

Wish I could have kissed you longer. See you tomorrow.

Damn! I hope he doesn't think I ignored him. I'll apologize in the morning since he's probably asleep now. Hunter shook his head then stood. He changed into his sleep shorts before crawling into bed.

After tucking his pillow under his head, he stared at the wall while listening to the water run in the other room. It would take Lonnie a while to shower. His friend liked using all the hot water he could. Hunter fell asleep to that sound.

* * * *

"Get your ass out of bed."

Hunter grunted when Lonnie punched him in the

shoulder. "What the hell? Why are you so mean in the morning?" He rubbed the spot and glared at Lonnie.

"I want coffee and pancakes. You're sleeping the day away. Besides, we have a tour to take of your possible new love interest's horse farm. I'll do my best to make myself scarce, so you can use your smooth moves on him." Nudging his hip, Lonnie winked at him.

"Shut the fuck up." Hunter climbed out of bed. "I'll go clean up then we can head to the café for..." He glanced at the clock. "Brunch. Did you text Andey and Scott?"

Lonnie was dressed already, but he flopped back on the mattress. "Yeah. Once we know the date, they'll join us a day or two before, so we can rehearse some of the new stuff. Did you text Boris?"

"Not yet. I'll do it after I'm done in the bathroom." Hunter headed toward the other room then paused. "Wait. The event isn't for a month. I wasn't planning on staying here the entire time. Don't we have gigs starting up in two weeks?"

"Yeah, but we'll come back a couple of days in advance of it to get the lay of the land and figure out exactly what Edward wants. I already checked our schedule. We don't have anything going on the weekend he wants us." Lonnie smiled. "Now get ready. I'm starving."

He did as Lonnie ordered him — he took a quick shower then dressed. Once he was done, Hunter gathered his wallet, room key and phone. He tapped Lonnie on the knee. "Let's get out of here."

After jumping to his feet, Lonnie led the way downstairs and out of the B&B. Hunter waited until they were making their way toward the café before pulling Edward's number up.

Sorry I missed your text. Got caught up in playing my guitar last night. Didn't hear my phone.

Hunter sent it, looking up to check he wasn't about to

walk into a pole or something, since he didn't trust Lonnie to watch out for him. The man would've thought it was hilarious. He was safe, so he scanned through for Boris' number then typed out a quick message.

Got a gig a month from now. A charity event. Will you be able to play?

A text popped up as they reached the café door. He followed Lonnie in and to the booth Rose pointed at. After dropping into the seat, he checked his phone then smiled. It was from Edward.

Wondered if that was why you didn't get back to me. Or maybe you just didn't want to talk to me.

Hunter snorted, but shook his head when Lonnie looked at him.

Oh, I want to talk to you. Want more than that actually. Still willing to let us invade your farm this afternoon?

Yes. I'll text you the directions. Come around two and I'll be able to give you a tour.

Awesome. See you in a couple hours.

Great. Looking forward to it.

He set his phone on the table and didn't bother looking at it when it vibrated because Rose had come over to take their order. When she left, he checked it and winced.

I'll be with you fuckers anyway.

Boris had gotten back to him. Sighing, he sent a smiley face to his friend, but nothing else. Sometimes it didn't pay to reply to Boris.

"What did Boris have to say?" Lonnie stared at him from across the table.

"How did you know it was from him?" He took a sip from his glass.

Lonnie snorted. "You always get a certain unhappy and exasperated look on your face when you're talking to him. So is he in?"

After clearing his throat, Hunter said, "I'll be with you fuckers anyway."

"Sounds exactly like something Boris would say." Lonnie rolled his eyes. "Do you have directions to Edward's place? Not that we couldn't get them from someone here."

Rose brought over their plates, setting them down before smiling. "Here you go, boys. Enjoy."

"Thanks, Rose." Hunter returned the smile then dug into his pancakes. "Yes. He sent them to me, so we're good. Edward said to come over around two."

Grunting, Lonnie picked up the syrup, drowning his own pancakes in it. When his plate was empty, Hunter leaned back against the back of the bench seat.

"That was great," he muttered as he reached for his coffee mug. "Might need to go for a run before we head out to Edward's or I'm going to get fat."

"Sounds like a plan to me. Hell, I've got to keep my body tight for all my wild fans. They don't go for the chubby singers." Lonnie chuckled.

Hunter eyed him. "I think you do well enough with the fans. You don't have to worry about it, but exercise is always a good thing, especially if we keep eating like this."

Lonnie waved Rose over. "We'd like our bill, please."

"Sure, honey. I have it right here." She held it out for him to take. "You can bring it up to the cash register when you're ready to go."

"Oh, do you know what kind of pie — or cake — Edward Monterrose likes?" Hunter asked.

"Yes, and we actually happen to have a fresh apple pie. I'll box it up for you." She patted his hand before she walked away.

"We're bringing him pie now? You're really taking the whole 'the way to a man's heart is through his stomach' adage literally," Lonnie joked while they headed up to the register.

Hunter shrugged. "My mom always says we should take a gift when we go to someone's house. I thought a pie would be nice, considering I don't know anything else about him."

After tugging out his wallet, Lonnie paid the bill. "You can pay me back for the pie later."

"Thanks." He took the box Rose handed him. "Let's go. Do you want to stop at the coffee shop to see Tad before we head back to the B&B?"

Lonnie pursed his lips then nodded. "Yeah. Probably should. Just to be nice."

"Maybe you can hook up with him again," Hunter commented, bumping their hips together.

"I told you that wasn't going to happen," Lonnie reminded him.

Shaking his head, Hunter replied, "I've heard that same old song a hundred times before, Lonnie. Tad's good looking and willing. Why not get some while you're here? It's not like he's expecting you to propose, right?"

He burst out laughing at Lonnie's rather horrified expression. Hunter shoved open the door to the coffee shop then gestured for Lonnie to go ahead of him. He spied Tad working the counter and grinned at the obvious happiness on the younger man's face.

Sure, neither of them were looking for anything serious, but that didn't mean Lonnie and Tad couldn't enjoy each other's company while Lonnie was in town. Hunter never quite got Lonnie's tendency for one-night stands. It made sense when they were touring and were only in a town for one gig and they left the next day, but if they were going to be in town for a week or so, Hunter didn't see the problem with spending more time with someone.

That's what he was kind of hoping for with Edward.

Whether their relationship ever moved beyond the fling it could be or not, Hunter was going to do his level best to get Edward in bed. *More than once, if I have anything to say about it.*

Chapter Seven

"Edward, there are two guys here to see you." Lisa peeked around the door of his office.

"Great. I'm expecting them." He pushed his chair back then stood, rubbing his left arm. He hadn't put the sling on that morning because the strap had irritated his neck, plus it hampered his ability to help with the horses. The bones were healing and as long as he didn't put a lot of weight on it or ride yet, he'd be fine.

Hunter and Lonnie walked in as he made his way to the door. He didn't think about it, just wrapped his arm around Hunter's waist then drew him close, pressing their lips together. He'd been thinking about the kiss they'd shared the day before.

Edward approved when Hunter opened to him. He swept his tongue in to stroke along Hunter's, teasing and tasting. Edging closer, Hunter entwined his arms around Edward's shoulders.

Coughing broke them apart and Edward turned to see Lonnie leaning against his desk, watching them.

"Very nice. Seems you missed each other more than you let on," Lonnie commented. "I'm impressed."

Hunter punched Lonnie in the arm. "Shut up, asshole. You didn't hear me making snarky remarks when you kissed Tad at the coffee shop. And about how you came home really late last night."

Lonnie rolled his eyes. "Jeez…have a little fun with a guy and he gets all violent. Also, I didn't kiss Tad nearly as all tongue-y as you did."

Edward chuckled. "All right, guys. Good to see you again,

Lonnie. I'm glad you could come out, though I'm thinking Tad is probably working the afternoon shift, right?"

"Yes, he is, but I didn't want Hunter coming out to some strange place with a guy he just met. I mean, a true friend doesn't let his buddy go off with strangers." Lonnie grinned.

"God, you're an ass." Hunter shook his head.

Lonnie winked. "I've been called that a lot. Usually by you."

After Hunter punched Lonnie again, Edward gestured to the chairs. "Would you like to sit or should I give you a tour of the training center? Then we can go over to my place, which is right next door."

"Oh, we brought you pie." Hunter pointed to the box sitting on Edward's desk. "Do you have some place to put it?"

He glanced at the logo and smiled. "Rose's apple pie, I bet. Thanks. I love her pies. I'll throw it in the fridge in the family area, then we'll go and look around."

Hunter and Lonnie followed him as he swept up the box before leading the way to the room next to the indoor arena. He'd had it built so parents could watch their kids during riding lessons when the weather was bad enough to ride indoors. It was heated and had a refrigerator stocked with drinks and snacks for everyone, not just the parents.

When Edward wrote his name on the top of the box, Hunter laughed. "Making sure no one takes your pie?"

"Of course. Rose's famous for her baking, which is why she's doing the desserts for my benefit." Edward smiled then slid the pie in the fridge. "Everyone would love to have a piece, but I'm not sharing. At least not right now. Let's take a walk."

"What's up with the break room?" Lonnie pointed back over his shoulder "Pretty swanky for your employees."

"They hang out there sometimes, but it's more for the parents who bring their kids for lessons. Or owners who want to watch their horses get worked." He shrugged. "I wanted them to have a place to relax, especially on days when it's too cold to really do anything outside. It's one of the luxuries of boarding your horse here."

Pursing his lips, Hunter nodded. "Sounds like a nice perk."

As they walked down the aisle of the barn, Edward patted the noses of some inquisitive horses checking out who was moving around.

"Why aren't these out like the rest of them?" Lonnie asked.

"They're the ones whose owners don't want them turned out in the paddocks or who are getting ready to head out to different shows on the East Coast." Edward took a clipboard off the wall at the front of the barn. "We keep a list of all the animals that are coming and going. On any given day, we have ten to fifteen horses heading out to different shows."

Hunter glanced at the twenty stalls in the main barn. "Are these the best horses you have here?"

Edward shook his head. "Some of them are at the top of their discipline. Eventing, jumping and dressage. There are a few who are do well in hunter classes and shows like that."

"Are any of them yours?" Lonnie winked at one of the young ladies walking her horse toward the outdoor arena.

"Girls or horses?" Edward joked.

Hunter snorted when Lonnie shot Edward a look. "I'm pretty sure he meant horses, but with Lonnie, you never know."

"Well, I don't have any children that I know of," Edward commented as he continued in the direction of the next barn. "My horses and those I'm training for clients are in this barn. I have ten in various stages of training. Again, some are competing at the highest level of jumping and dressage. Others are working their way up to the Grand Prix level."

They strolled through the barn, but his horses were out in the paddocks as none were scheduled for a show that weekend. Well, all of them were out except for Salt, who had just returned from Les' refresher course. Edward had planned on flying out to work with him, but Les had been called away on business, so it had been easier just to bring Salt home. He intended to get back in the saddle tomorrow, even though his doctor advised him to wait another week.

He wandered over to where Salt hung his head over his stall door. "This is my main star, Gypsy's Salty Liar. His sire was the first Grand Prix-level horse I owned and trained on my own. One of the best damn horses I ever rode. Salt has the same talent, if I can get him over his irrational fear of water jumps."

Shaking his head, Salt snorted as though he understood what Edward said and disagreed.

"He just returned from a trip out to Wyoming where a friend of mine was helping him remember how water won't hurt him. The vet's coming to check him out then we'll resume our training tomorrow."

"Umm...aren't you still injured?" Hunter touched Edward's shoulder lightly. "Doesn't seem like the wisest decision to get back on when you could do more damage."

He covered Hunter's hand then squeezed. "You don't understand horse people, do you? We don't have a lot of patience if it doesn't involve horses. As long as I can ride, I will. I've had to take two weeks off before getting back in the saddle. Hell, if I hadn't been so bruised and hadn't broken a couple of ribs, I would've gotten back on the next day. A broken collarbone and wrist are painful, but I've ridden with worse."

"Worse?" Lonnie frowned. "I've done gigs with sprained ankles and shit, but never tried to ride a horse with one."

Edward ran his hand down Salt's nose. "I've ridden with broken ankles, twisted knees, sprained wrists and various other injuries. As dangerous as it sounds, I'm willing to take the chance of a serious injury when it comes to competing and giving my horses a chance to show how talented they are."

Hunter edged closer to Edward's side then held out his

hand out so Salt could sniff it. "Have you ever had a really serious injury?"

"You mean like career—or life—threatening?" At Hunter's nod, Edward shook his head. "I've been lucky so far. One of my closest friends, Les, was in an accident while at a show. His horse slipped while taking off for a jump. Les wasn't ready for it, so he fell off. Sam kicked him in the head, though it could've been worse."

He smiled slightly when both men shot him incredulous looks. "No, really. Sam could've landed directly on him, crushing his skull. Somehow, the horse managed to twist his body enough to, basically, graze Les' skull. Les was in a coma for a while then when he woke up, he had to relearn everything. Had to quit competing. So I'm aware that it happens and I'm always as careful as I can be."

Lonnie nodded. "But accidents happen sometimes. There's no way of avoiding them."

Edward agreed, which was why he took all the precautions in the world, but he wasn't going to spend any more time on the sidelines than necessary. He gave Salt one more pat before strolling out of the barn. He showed Hunter and Lonnie around the rest of the training center then took them over to his farm.

"This is my breeding operation and my home. This farm went up for sale a few years ago. At the time, I was thinking about retiring Gypsy. He was getting older and I didn't want to risk him getting injured. He's a stallion and a Grand Prix-level jumper with a lot of wins under his belt, so to speak. I'd had people inquire about breeding their mares to him, so I took a chance on starting up my own operation." Edward gestured to some foals frolicking in one of the paddocks, their mothers watching over them. "It's turned out to be pretty successful."

He took them through the foaling barn, the yearling barn and the barn where the mares and their foals were kept. Also, the stallion barn and the smaller barn where his retired horses stayed. The ones who couldn't bear offspring and those he'd retired from competition. There were a couple of ponies there as well. Lonnie fell in love with the little Shetland pony that Edward had adopted to keep his retired geldings company while they adjusted to not working anymore.

Hunter laughed as Lonnie scratched the pony's chin and cooed at him. "I've never seen him like this before. It's kind of creepy."

"Lonnie, be careful. He's grumpy and will bite if you don't watch him," Edward warned then turned to look at Hunter. "Some people love ponies, and I see their merit, but I have yet to meet one that isn't stubborn and ornery at times. Maybe you can take him out on tour with you."

"Oh, I don't think so," Hunter protested. "We have two vans. One for our equipment and crap. The other is for the humans. We don't have any room for a pony."

"Maybe a goat then." Edward gestured for them to follow. "I have a couple of those as well."

He led them to the closet paddock then whistled. He grinned when he saw Gypsy come pounding up from the far end. Mud covered the stallion from head to tail, along with pieces of grass stuck here and there. He didn't back off when Gypsy dashed up then pushed his head against Edward's white polo.

Hunter cringed. "Not sure that's going to wash out, man."

Edward looked down at the smears of mud, horse snot and grass stains on the front of his shirt. "If I wanted to look perfect all the time, I wouldn't work with horses. They don't care about looking good. This is Gypsy's Salt Mine, my very first top-level horse, and the foundation stallion of my breeding program."

Scratching Gypsy's favorite spot on his neck, Edward watched Hunter hold out his hand for Gypsy to sniff. The stallion lipped Hunter softly and Edward pulled a peppermint out of his pocket, unwrapping it before setting it on Hunter's palm.

"This is what he really wants. As long as you bring him

these, he'll be your friend for life."

Gypsy snatched the mint away then munched on it, happy to let Edward and Hunter pet him. After joining them, Lonnie pointed to the little black creature standing next to Gypsy.

"What's that?"

"Oh, that's Scooby, Gypsy's best friend. They shared a stall and this paddock. I got him when I retired Gypsy, who'd get all worked up when he saw the other horses loading onto the trailers to leave for a show. I thought he might like having a companion to hang out with. The goat's smart. The moment the first truck pulls into the driveway, he does his best to distract Gypsy. We've usually got the horses loaded and everything ready to go before Gypsy notices." Bending, Edward patted the goat's head. "Just be careful. This one will chew on your shoes, jacket or anything else you leave within his reach."

"The stories about goats eating anything are true, huh?" Lonnie crouched to get a closer look at Scooby.

Edward shrugged. "I don't know about that. He's never got as far as eating anything he shouldn't, but he's chewed up a lot of stuff. Ruined some expensive reins before we learned to put everything up out of his reach."

"That's really what we need on our tour. He'd chew the shit out of all the cords," Lonnie muttered. "But he is cute."

"Hey, Edward."

He turned to see Juan striding toward him from the direction of the training arena. Stepping away from the fence, he held out his hand.

"Juan, how's Yancey doing?"

Juan shook his hand while nodding at Hunter and Lonnie. "He didn't break anything. Thank God. Just going to be very sore for a little while. He's already complaining, since the doctor told him he had to take two days off work."

"He just takes a page from your book. Remember how whiny you get when you're laid up for even a day," Edward joked. "Glad to hear it was nothing serious."

"So am I. I just wanted to let you know I'm here for the rest of the day. You won't need to do anything with my clients today, though I would like to hear your thoughts about the ones you worked with yesterday." Juan glanced at Hunter and Lonnie. "I'll catch you tomorrow morning."

Edward motioned to Hunter. "Hunter Lee. Lonnie Balet. This is Juan Romanos. He's one of my most talented former students, plus one of the best riders on the show circuit. Also, he's a pretty good trainer as well."

Hunter and Lonnie shook Juan's hand. Edward could see his friend eyeing both men. *He's probably trying to figure out which one I'm interested in, since neither of them really look like horse people.*

"I've known Edward since I was eighteen. Met him through my uncle and one of my uncle's best friends. He's a good man." Juan slapped Edward on his good shoulder. "I'll see you tomorrow. Are you going to call it a day? I'll let everyone know to call your place if they need you."

"Yes. Thanks. That would be great."

Lonnie whimpered slightly when Juan walked away. "Wow. That is a prime example of male perfection."

Edward laughed. "Juan is pretty good looking, but he's also taken. He and his husband, Yancey, met when they were teenagers and have been in love ever since. They're perfect for each other."

"Figures," Lonnie murmured. "All the good ones are taken."

Hunter bumped his friend with his hip. "I thought you weren't looking for anything serious?"

"I'm not, but it doesn't mean I can shop around and try some on to see if they fit." Lonnie frowned when Hunter snorted. "Shut up, asshole."

Edward took Hunter's hand. "Why don't I show you my house? We can talk a little more about the benefit. Maybe you can give me an idea of what songs you'll be playing? I think I have one of Derek's old guitars around somewhere."

Hunter's eyes widened and Edward figured it must be

kind of a special thing for him to get to use Derek's guitar. It was weird when he saw how excited others got when they had a chance to meet Derek. Oh, he knew his brother was famous and looked up to, but all Edward ever saw was Derek, his brother and the only family he loved.

"He wouldn't mind if I used it?" Hunter walked next to him as they wandered up to his small cottage-style home.

"No. If it was one of his favorite instruments, he'd never have left it behind. He did it so he would always have one here just in case inspiration struck and he wanted to write a song." He opened the door then ushered them into the mudroom. "Just leave your shoes and jackets here."

Chapter Eight

Hunter kicked off his boots then hung up his jacket. He followed Edward into a spacious kitchen. Black countertops went well with the dark wood cabinets. There was a large island in the middle that Edward gestured to.

"Would you like something to drink?" Edward asked as he headed for the refrigerator.

Lonnie flopped onto one of the stools before propping his elbows on the top. "Sure. You got any soda?"

"Yes. What about you, Hunter?" Edward shot him a glance from over his shoulder.

"I'd take some iced tea if you've got any." Hunter took the seat next to Lonnie, but kept looking around. The kitchen gleamed and Hunter wondered how often Edward cooked in it. To be honest, it didn't look like the space got used very often.

After setting two glasses in front of them, Edward leaned back by the sink.

"This kitchen is nice," Lonnie commented after taking a sip of his drink. "Do you really use it or is it all for show?"

Hunter wanted to punch him in the arm, though he was secretly happy his friend had asked the question. Edward's plump lips curved into a smile.

"I can really cook. My cleaning lady was in earlier today, which is why everything is nice and shiny. Usually by this time every week, the house is a complete wreck. I'm busy with the horses and my clients — I don't have time to be neat. At least not in my own home." Edward straightened. "Do you want to see the rest of the place? It's not very big, but since it's just me, I don't need that much space. Besides,

I spend more time out in the barns than I do here."

Hunter and Lonnie picked up their glasses then trailed along behind Edward as he gave them a tour of his house. The living room had a large bay window that faced the paddocks. Hunter imagined how nice it must be to sit on the couch and watch the foals play while their mothers grazed. Edward's home office didn't hold trophies as Hunter had thought it would. There were a lot of pictures on the walls and the bookshelves as well. When he snuck a peek at one, he saw Edward standing with his arm around the shoulders of a tall, dark-haired man, who he recognized as Derek St. Martin.

One of the other pictures caught his eye and he wandered over to look at it while Lonnie asked Edward questions about one of the few trophies that sat on his desk. Edward was much younger in the photo. He wasn't facing the camera—his gaze was focused on the painfully thin blonde woman next to him. She probably wasn't much older than Edward, but there was a lot of pain in her blue eyes.

"Samantha," Edward said softly, causing Hunter to jump.

He'd been so intent on the photo, he hadn't heard Edward approach him. "Who was she?"

"My first love. I met her at the stable where I took riding lessons when I was sixteen. God, she was beautiful and funny and the nicest girl I'd ever met." Edward lifted the frame from the shelf and smiled.

Hunter saw sadness in Edward's eyes. "What happened? Are you still friends?"

Edward shook his head. "No. She died when we were eighteen. Developed bone cancer and there wasn't anything the doctors could do for her. Her parents and I tried to make her last months perfect. We took her to Paris and all the other places she'd wanted to visit. Hardest thing I ever had to do was watch her die."

"I'm sorry." Hunter rested his hand on Edward's arm then squeezed. "Loving anyone opens us up to getting hurt."

"Yes, it does." Edward returned the photo.

"You kissed Hunter in the park. So you're an equal opportunity lover," Lonnie joked.

Hunter blushed when Edward shot him a glance. "I just told him we kissed. I didn't give any details."

"I'm bisexual. I've had relationships with men and women. I like them equally." Edward motioned to the door. "Would you like to see the other rooms?"

Lonnie opened his mouth to say something else, but Hunter grabbed him then dragged him out. He wanted to shake Lonnie for trying to embarrass Edward. While Hunter didn't totally understand liking both men and women, he wasn't about to question Edward about his preferences. He was going to assume that no matter who Edward was in a relationship with, he was in it a hundred percent.

Idiot. I'm not even in a relationship with him. One kiss doesn't a commitment make. Hunter mentally rolled his eyes. *Let's not make things more serious than they are.*

The master bedroom was huge and done in dark blues and greens. Hunter found it rather soothing. Like in the living room, the windows looked out over the paddocks. He moved to stand by one, staring down into a paddock where a dark brown mare—at least he assumed it was a mare—and a black foal raced around. Well, the foal raced around his mother in widening circles while she calmly grazed.

Warmth engulfed him and he realized Edward had come to stand behind him, resting one of his hands on Hunter's hip. Without thinking, Hunter leaned back into Edward's solid body. There was never any doubt that Edward could support his weight. He swallowed a moan when Edward slid his hand around to rest on Hunter's stomach, somehow finding his way under Hunter's shirt.

"That's one of Gypsy's foals. I own his dam, so he'll stay here for now. I don't sell a lot of Gypsy's offspring until I know they're trained right and I can find just the right owner for them. I'm very protective of them," Edward whispered. "Like they were my own children."

Hunter shuddered at the moist heat bathing his ear. His cock stiffened and he was pretty sure that if Edward glanced down, he'd be able to see the bulge in Hunter's jeans. Then Edward shifted closer, letting Hunter know he wasn't the only one affected by their closeness.

"Hey, I think I'm going to head back into town. I told Tad I'd take him out to dinner tonight," Lonnie said.

They eased away from each other, then Hunter turned to face Lonnie. His friend simply lifted an eyebrow at him before turning to Edward.

"Thanks for the tour. I really enjoyed it. I can't wait to come back." Lonnie clapped Edward on the back. "I'll see myself out."

"You're welcome to come any time, Lonnie. Just give me a call and if I'm not available, I'll make sure someone else is." Edward sounded a little hoarse. "Are you sure you want to leave? I thought we could have dinner or something."

"Nah. Like I said, I have a date with Tad." Lonnie wiggled his eyebrows. "Don't expect me home tonight."

Hunter chuckled. "I never expect you home when you've met someone. I'll text you later."

"Don't have too much fun, guys." Lonnie waved then disappeared down the hall toward the front door.

Edward smiled. "I didn't mean to run him off."

"Oh, I think he's been trying to figure out a way to get us alone since we arrived. I mean, he did want to see the place, but he also wanted to give us a chance to build on the kiss." Hunter took a deep breath before edging forward to wrap his arms around Edward's waist. He pulled him tight against his body then pressed their lips together.

The heavy weight of Edward's cast rested at the small of Hunter's back, but he didn't mind. All he was thinking about was the way Edward's mouth fit his and how the man tasted as he swept his tongue inside. Humming, he gripped Edward's ass, loving how firm it was.

Edward moaned then broke their kiss by tilting his head. Hunter didn't complain too much since it gave him access to Edward's neck. He licked a line along the strong jaw down to the hollow of Edward's throat where he sucked up a small mark.

"I think we should lie down," Edward muttered. "I'm still not a hundred percent."

"I don't want to hurt you," Hunter murmured. "Maybe we shouldn't do anything."

His knees hit the side of the bed and he flailed as Edward pushed him onto it. Laughing, Edward began taking his own clothes off. Hunter didn't want to be left out, so he sat up before tugging his shirt over his head.

"Oh, I have plans for us," Edward said. "And they don't include us skipping sex. I just have to be cautious, but I think we can have fun. Do you like top or bottom?"

"Either works for me." Hunter tossed his shirt to the side then started on his jeans.

Edward slid his tight tan pants down his muscular legs, turning slightly as he bent to remove them. Hunter almost swallowed his tongue at the bubble butt right there in front of him. He forgot about his own clothes, reaching out to cup those firm globes. He smiled when Edward squeaked slightly in surprise.

"Your hands are a little cold." Edward pushed back into his grip. "You need to let go of me, so I can get naked without falling and breaking something else. It wouldn't look good at the hospital."

Hunter burst out laughing as the image of Edward being rolled into the emergency room, totally naked and trying to explain how he broke his nose, played in his head.

"Thanks for the support, Hunter. I'd tell all of them it was your fault. You distracted me and I tripped over the pants around my ankles." Edward winked. "I have no shame. Nothing embarrasses me."

"You haven't hung out with Lonnie long enough. Just wait. He'll do something to cause you to blush or want to kill him. It's a toss-up most of the time." Hunter traced a line along Edward's crease, pausing for a second to rub his thumb over Edward's puckered hole.

Edward whimpered then cleared his throat. "I'd prefer not to talk about your friend while we're naked. He's not the one I want in my bed."

Hunter leaned forward to place an open-mouthed kiss on one cheek. He pinched the other and got back to getting the rest of his clothes off. Once he was naked, he held out his hand. "Come on then."

He helped Edward crawl onto the bed then lay beside him. They faced each other, doing nothing but touching fingertips to skin. Hunter caressed the fading yellow bruises along Edward's left side. He winced at a darker one on Edward's hip.

"That one looks like it really hurt," he commented, wiggling around so he could place a soft kiss on it.

"I was quite sore for a week or so afterward, but I'm healing. I will say it is hell getting older. I don't recover as fast as I did before." Edward traced a thin scar running the length of Hunter's forearm. "What happened here?"

Hunter lifted his arm, holding it to the evening twilight coming through the windows. "I know what it looks like, but that's not it. I didn't try to kill myself. It was a freak accident one night while Boris and I were setting up for a gig. I tripped over a cord and tried to catch myself on a glass-top table. I hit the corner just right. It sliced my arm almost from elbow to wrist. Thank God Boris was there. He got a bandage on it then drove me to the hospital."

Wincing, Edward copied Hunter's gesture, brushing his lips over the scar. "Did you play the gig?"

"We had to postpone it a couple of days, but yeah, I did the gig. I was lucky it was my left arm. Less stress put on it." Hunter smirked. "The show must go on."

"And you were harassing me about getting back on my horses with a broken wrist." Edward poked him in the side. "It's all the same, honey. I have to ride if I want to keep my ranking. Also, if I want to get to the big shows, I need the points for me and my horses."

Hunter nodded. He understood pushing oneself to be the best in whatever he did. "Okay. How did we get off topic like this? I thought we were going to have sex."

Not saying a word, Edward grabbed Hunter then rolled on his back. Hunter found himself lying on top of Edward, naked chest to naked chest. Their bodies fit together and he groaned as Edward spread his legs to let him settle between them.

"God, you feel so good against me," he murmured into Edward's ear then bit his earlobe.

A shudder raced through Edward and Hunter could see the goosebumps on his skin. *He likes that. Let's see what else he likes.* He eased down Edward's body, placing kisses and nibbles along the way to see which spots got a reaction from his lover. He discovered Edward's nipples were rather sensitive, so he spent a little more time on them.

Edward entwined his fingers in Hunter's hair then tugged gently. "You need to find somewhere else to play, or I'll be coming and I don't want that. It'll take me a while to get it up again. I want the first time to be with you inside me."

Hunter shivered at the thought of sliding his cock into Edward and decided he liked that idea. "All right."

He licked from the center of Edward's chest to his belly button where he dipped his tongue in and Edward squirmed. *Edward's ticklish. I'll have to explore that at some other time.* Of course, he was getting ahead of himself, thinking there might be another time after this. For all he knew, Edward was thinking of a one-night stand instead of a longer relationship.

Giving himself a mental slap, Hunter realized at that moment it didn't matter what Edward had planned for them. All that mattered was making sure Edward enjoyed himself and came while Hunter got his rocks off.

He hit the head of Edward's cock with his chin. It left a trace of pre-cum on his skin. After swiping it away with his hand, Hunter pushed farther down until he was face-to-face—so to speak—with Edward's shaft. It wasn't as long as Hunter's but it was thick and he couldn't wait to feel it inside his own ass. But that was for later.

After wrapping his hand around the base, he ran his tongue along the entire length before pressing his tongue into Edward's slit.

"Oh fuck." Edward arched his back, pushing into Hunter's face.

"That will be happening eventually," Hunter said before he took Edward in as far as he could. He applied suction, bobbing up and down, working the length of flesh in his mouth. He matched the pumping of his fist with his head to give Edward the maximum pleasure.

He didn't stop Edward from thrusting, just took each stroke in until his shaft hit the back of his throat then he swallowed around it. Edward moaned and groaned, obviously not able to verbalize what he was feeling. Hunter didn't mind, since it was plain that Edward was enjoying what he was doing.

Not wanting to stop, he slipped two of his fingers into his mouth alongside Edward's cock and got them as wet as he could. Hunter took them out before he reached down to tease Edward's hole.

"God! Please," Edward begged, trying to lift his hips and give Hunter more access.

Taking advantage of the move, Hunter slowly invaded Edward's ass with his fingers. He stretched and did his best to relax Edward's inner channel while continuing to pleasure Edward using his mouth.

Chapter Nine

Pressure built behind Edward's balls and he balanced on the edge of coming. He tapped Hunter's shoulder, hoping to get his attention. When he looked up and his lust-filled gaze hit Edward's, it was almost too much. Biting his lip, he used the sting to back off a little.

"You need to fuck me now, Hunter. I'm so close," he told him. "There are condoms and lube in a basket under the bed. I tossed them there before you came over."

There was no reason not to let Hunter know how eager he'd been for this to happen. He whimpered when Hunter moved away. He missed his fingers, his mouth and his body. Lying back on the pillows, he watched as Hunter dug out the battered bottle of lube and a strip of condoms.

"I'm not sure we'll get through all those tonight," he joked.

Hunter winked. "You never know."

When Hunter settled back between his thighs, Edward grabbed his leg behind the knee then brought it up and out. He couldn't do it with his left leg since his wrist was still in a cast, but he doubted it would matter. The rustle of the foil packet caught his attention and he looked down to see Hunter tear it open.

Edward laughed softly when Hunter's eyes crossed as he rolled the condom down the length of his cock. He imagined it was quite sensitive right at the moment. It was hard, long and thick, just as Edward liked. He couldn't wait to take Hunter in.

Hunter squirted slick on the palm of his hand before tossing the bottle to the floor. He coated his shaft then rubbed the excess around Edward's opening. They stared into each other's eyes while Hunter positioned himself.

"Here we go," Hunter murmured and Edward nodded, giving him silent permission.

He let his head fall back as the pressure of Hunter invading his ass built until he popped past the ring of muscles and sank deep. He inhaled deeply, focusing on relaxing his body. Then the need for more took over and he moved just a little so Hunter knew he could as well.

Hunter grunted as he began thrusting in and out, at first slow and easy, but as time went by, he grew faster and rougher. Edward rocked in perfect counterpoint to Hunter's rhythm. His shouts filled the room each time Hunter nailed his gland.

Suddenly his climax exploded through him. He cried out, "Hunter!" His cum covered his stomach, some even reaching his chest. Edward trembled as desire rocketed along his nerves. "Fuck!"

His orgasm drove Hunter over the edge and he slammed into Edward one last time before freezing as he filled the rubber. Edward did everything he could to draw out their climaxes until Hunter collapsed on top of him.

At least he had enough presence of mind to fall on Edward's right side, avoiding most of his healing bones. Edward smoothed back Hunter's sweat-soaked hair while trying to calm his racing heart. Finally, when their breathing had evened out, Hunter rolled off him onto the bed.

He stared up at the ceiling while Hunter shuffled to the bathroom. Edward assumed he was taking care of the condom and cleaning up. He had to do that as well, but he felt too good to move at the moment.

"Here." Hunter sat on the mattress beside him then wiped off his stomach with a damp washcloth. "How about we take a nap then figure out something for dinner?"

Edward yawned. "Sounds like a great idea, but I have to call down to the barns first. I want to make sure everything is all right." He took the cloth from Hunter then tossed it in the general vicinity of the bathroom.

"Sure. If you want, we can check it all out after our nap before we grab food?"

"I'd appreciate it. Juan would yell at me and tell me that I have good people working for me. I don't need to be so micromanaging, but I just like knowing everything's all right." Edward grinned then wiggled under the blankets and Hunter joined him.

"I don't blame you, man. Not knowing might lead to surprises and you don't need those. I'm kind of the same way with the band. I want to make sure everything is perfect—or as perfect as humanly possible. It's my livelihood. Same as you." Hunter snuggled close, resting his head on Edward's shoulder.

Closing his eyes, Edward nodded. "Horses are amazing creatures, but they can get sick—or injured—so easily. One hour, they're fine and running around. The next time you check on them, they're down with colic. Which is why I like to look at each one several times throughout the day. Might catch something before it gets serious."

Hunter mumbled something, but Edward couldn't understand the words, so he just drifted along on the sound of Hunter's breathing.

* * * *

The buzzing of his phone woke Edward up later. He smacked himself with his cast when he went to scrub his left hand over his face.

"Shit," he swore as he struggled to get out from under the covers. He glanced over to where Hunter had been sleeping, but that side of the bed was empty.

Stumbling across the room, he managed to get to his phone before the ringing stopped. He didn't even check the ID, simply answered.

"Hello?"

"Hey there, bro. How are you?" Derek's cheerful voice

assaulted his eardrum.

"Ugh!" Edward slid down his dresser to sit on the floor.

Derek snorted. "That doesn't sound good. Are you in pain? Get back to riding too soon?"

"I'll have you know that I haven't ridden yet. That's for tomorrow." He scratched his stomach and yawned.

"Did I wake you up?" Derek sounded shocked. "It's only what? Six your time? What are you doing taking a nap? You never nap, not even when you're laid up."

Edward debated lying to his brother, but decided it wasn't worth all the crap he'd get if Derek found out he had. Besides, he had a feeling Derek would be happy to hear Edward had slept with someone.

"I was enjoying a post-sex nap, if you really need to know."

He held the phone away from his ear while Derek shouted. After waiting until the noise had died down, he returned it to hear Derek say, "I can't believe you finally got some."

"Christ! You make it sound like I'm a virgin. You do know I've been having sex since I was fifteen, right?" Annoyance colored his tone.

"I know, but you haven't had anyone in your bed for a couple months now." Derek chuckled.

Edward sighed. "Just because they weren't in my bed doesn't mean I wasn't fucking people. Besides, I've been busy with shows, horses and clients. It's not like I joined a convent or something. Plus I don't have to tell you every time I have sex, Derek."

He heard Derek grunt then the Australian-accented voice of Derek's husband, Max. "Stop teasing your brother, love. He doesn't give you a hard time about your sex life anymore. Let him be."

"Yeah, let me be. Since you and Max hooked up, I haven't harassed you hardly at all about what you two do in bed." Edward could admit Derek and Max made a fantasy-inducing couple, but he wasn't about to imagine them in bed together.

"All right. I'll stop for now, but when we show up in a week or two, you'd better be ready to spill. Will you be seeing this person again?"

Smiling at how Derek didn't use pronouns, Edward decided to throw him a bone. "I'm hoping Hunter will agree to seeing each other again. He's in a band and on the road a lot, so it'll take some arranging to figure it out."

Derek hummed softly then asked, "A band, huh? How the hell did you meet him?"

"His band just got off touring up and down the East Coast. He's vacationing in town and I saw him playing in the park. I liked his music so I approached him. Things went from there."

"Is the band any good?"

His question didn't surprise Edward. Derek was always looking for fresh new talent. "I think they are. I'll text you the name and you can check them out online. Plus you'll see them at the benefit. I asked them to be your opening act. In addition to that, they'll play throughout the night."

Derek was quiet for a second. Finally he said, "Yeah, send me their name. I'll check them out. Aside from being exhausted because you finally got some, how are you feeling? Bones healing well?"

The door opened and he looked to see Hunter peering in. He frowned when he spotted Edward on the floor. Edward motioned to the phone, but held out his hand when Hunter offered him a coffee mug.

"Everything's healing on schedule. Doctors haven't cleared me to ride yet, but that's never stopped me before. Of course, I might regret the extracurricular activities in the morning." He grinned at Hunter, who rolled his eyes.

"Great. I hadn't heard from you a couple of days, so I thought I'd check in. I don't want to take you away from your friend. Give me a call later in the week. Love you, man."

"Love you too, Derek. Give Max a hug for me. I'm looking forward to seeing him in a couple of weeks." Edward ended the call then let his phone drop to the floor beside his knee. He took a sip of coffee before he asked, "How long have you been up?"

Hunter crouched in front of him. "Only about twenty minutes. Thought I'd make some coffee and check on the rest of the guys. I try to do that once a day, just to make sure they're not getting into too much trouble."

"Well, you know what Lonnie's doing tonight. Are the others as likely to be doing the same sort of thing?" He handed his mug back to Hunter before pushing to his feet. "Let me get dressed then we can go do bed check for the horses and see if anyone's still around."

Hunter settled in the chair after setting Edward's mug on the nightstand. "Well, Andey and Scott are best friends. They're always hanging out together. They do get into trouble, but it's usually nothing bad that they couldn't get out of. Boris is the one we're all worried about."

Edward frowned while he pulled on a pair of faded jeans. "Right. Boris is the guy who heads to New York and disappears. You're never sure what he does while he's away."

"Yeah. He always comes back so used up." Hunter glared down into his mug as though he thought it would show him Boris. "We all take off after tours because we need time away to relax and recharge, you know? But it's like he needs the tours to recover from whatever goes on when he's in New York."

"Have you ever followed him?" Edward grabbed a Henley out of his closet then got some socks from his dresser.

Hunter shook his head. "Boris told us if he ever found out we'd done that, he'd never come back."

Edward winced. "That's harsh. Doesn't he get that you're worried about him?"

"Sure he does, and it annoys the shit out of him when I text him to make sure he's still alive." Hunter shrugged. "I'm not taking the risk that he'll do what he says."

"I guess you're right. If he does disappear, you might

not be able to find him again. Does he do drugs?" Edward stood then picked up his coffee.

Hunter joined him by the door. "He doesn't do them while he's with us. The hardest stuff we do anymore is drink. Don't get me wrong, we all tried drugs when we were younger, but I figured out rather quick that it does nothing except fuck me up. The others don't do it around me. I know Lonnie is clean and I'm pretty sure Andey and Scott don't take any. I can't say for sure with Boris."

Edward led the way to the kitchen where he refilled his and Hunter's mugs. After that, they went to the mudroom and put on their boots and jackets.

"We'll go to the training center first. Grab the pie, if someone hasn't eaten it yet. Then come back and check on the horses here. I have people who work the night shift, making sure everything's fine. I'll make one more walk through around ten, then I head to bed. Have to get up early." He gestured in the direction of the training barns.

"Did you want me to go home after dinner?" Hunter touched his arm. "I don't want to screw up your routine."

Stopping, he covered Hunter's hand with his and smiled. "I was kind of hoping you'd stay tonight. Just because I have to get up early doesn't mean you do. You can sleep in and when you're ready to head back to town, you can come find me. I'll drive you. It'll give me a chance to double check with Rose about the desserts."

Hunter's face lit with happiness. "Cool. Then let's get this show on the road. I'm starving."

Chuckling, Edward continued on. He saw Juan's truck and another car parked in front of the indoor arena. It was dark out, so if Juan had a client, they'd be inside. Some of the horses were skittish about being outside at night, though Edward did keep a few of them in their paddocks through the nights until it got too cold.

He wandered down the aisle, stopping to visually check each horse. Hunter stayed by his side, but didn't say anything while Edward crooned to the animals. They all looked in the peak of health, with shiny coats and bright eyes. After going into his office, he grabbed the files Maria, his head assistant trainer, had left on his desk. He'd read them after dinner and see what remarks she'd made about the horses and their riders. He had already written up his notes on the students he'd instructed earlier in the day before Hunter had arrived.

Spotting Juan's jacket hanging on the coat rack in the corner, Edward left the door unlocked. Juan had a key and would make sure it was secure before he left. Edward took Hunter's hand then strolled over to the arena where he heard Juan talking. As they got there, he noticed a man leaning against the gate watching Juan.

"Hey, Yancey, glad to see you're no worse for wear after that cow kicked you," he commented as they approached. Edward gave Yancey a cautious hug, knowing from experience how sore the man probably was.

"Thanks, Edward. I'm just lucky it missed anything vital. Juan needed to get some extra work on Dolly, so I told him I'd meet him here then we're heading into town for dinner." Yancey eyed Hunter. "Did you two want to join us?"

"Yancey MacCafferty, this Hunter Lee. Hunter, this is Juan's husband, Yancey. He's my vet and has a practice down the road from here," Edward introduced them. "Maybe next time, Yancey."

Chapter Ten

"Nice meeting you," Hunter said as he shook Yancey's hand. He studied the man then glanced over to where Juan rode a beautiful gray mare. It probably would've sounded strange if he said it out loud, but Hunter could almost sense the couple's connection, even with the distance between them.

"You too." Yancey smiled at him then faced Edward. "You look like you're moving better. Getting back on a horse tomorrow, huh?"

Edward grinned. "How'd you guess?"

Yancey gestured toward Edward's left arm. "No sling. Remember, I know all about men who can't wait long enough to heal properly. You're nothing special, Monterrose. Hell, Juan and his uncle are shining examples of idiocy. The only one with enough sense is Les."

"Hey, don't be talking shit like that about my uncle Tony," Juan yelled from the center of the arena.

"Tony was crazy. All those injuries he had and he still rode. He had a death wish." Yancey turned to Hunter. "Juan's uncle Tony rode bulls for a living. He's retired now, but I'm sure there were times when he risked dying if he landed wrong."

Hunter lifted his shoulder in an abbreviated shrug. "I personally think anyone who rides bulls is certifiable or has a death wish, like you said. It takes a lot of balls to get on the back of a one-ton animal with just a rope to hold on to."

Both of the men with him nodded. Yancey went back to leaning on the gate while Edward watched Juan canter his mare in a circle before straightening her then moving toward a white three-rail fence. It looked huge to Hunter, but he was pretty sure it was considered small by Juan's and Edward's standards.

"She's going to refuse," Edward said softly.

Yancey grunted his agreement.

Sure enough, a few steps before the fence, Dolly planted her front feet and stopped. She shook her head and flicked her tail, annoyance obvious in every line of her body. Juan didn't seem to be angry with her. He simply turned her away from the jump then cantered her down to the other end of the arena.

"How did you know she wouldn't jump it?" Hunter hadn't seen any sign the horse wouldn't do what she was asked.

"Part of it is experience. After riding a lot of horses over the years, I have almost a sixth sense when it comes to that. It doesn't always work and my fall off Salt is a prime example." Edward motioned to Juan. "I guarantee Juan knew as well that she wasn't taking off. Because the other part of it is being in tune with your mount. Feeling every step she takes and every twitch of her muscles. How she carries herself as she approaches the jump."

Yancey flapped his hand in Edward's direction. "Besides Juan, Edward is the best rider I've seen at getting the most out of a horse. The reason Dolly stopped was because she didn't have the confidence to take the jump. She's only six years old and Juan is just starting to take her to shows. From where we stand on the ground, the jump looks big, but it's not in the grand scheme of what she'll eventually be asked to clear. It's only around three-feet-six-inches high, which is considered beginner level. Especially with the bloodline Dolly has."

Hunter found himself fascinated by everything the two men were telling him. As he'd told Edward, he'd always liked horses, but he'd never known all the work that went into training them. It sounded as though it were a lot harder than he'd thought it would be. Of course, he should've considered that, since the rider was working with a thousand-pound animal that had a mind of its own. If a horse didn't want to do something, there was no way a human could overpower it.

Juan had taken the mare over a few poles lying on the ground then over a very small cross-rail before bringing her back in line with the white-railed jump. Hunter tensed as they approached, but as he focused on Dolly's ears and the way she held her neck, he could tell she wasn't comfortable. He wasn't surprised when she ducked out at the last second.

"Juan," Edward called as he handed the folders he'd been carrying to Hunter. "Would you mind if I got on her? Maybe I can figure out what's causing her to do this."

"Fine by me. It might be as simple as she's a mare with her own mind and quirks." Juan steered Dolly over to the gate before he dismounted. He took off his riding helmet, handing it to Edward. "Here, you can use this. Hold her while I get the mounting block. You're not ready to be mounting from the ground."

Yancey saw the frown on Hunter's face. "It would put too much pressure on his wrist and collarbone," he explained.

Hunter edged closer to Yancey. "He really shouldn't be riding, should he?"

"No, but I've learned it's useless to try to convince them. To be honest, they know their bodies better than the doctors, so if he truly didn't think he could, Edward wouldn't ride." Yancey accepted a quick kiss from Juan before he went to help Edward.

"You said Les was the only one who had any sense about his injuries," Hunter commented. "Why is that?"

"Has Edward mentioned Les to you?"

They watched as Edward mounted Dolly, settling into the saddle with a sigh of contentment. Once he'd adjusted his stirrups to the right length, he gave Dolly a soft nudge with his heels to get her moving.

"Yes. He said Les retired because of an injury."

Yancey raised his eyebrows. "It was a life-threatening

injury, as well as career-ending. Yet I've known men — bull riders and horsemen — who ignore what the doctors say and go back to what got them injured in the first place. Once he recovered as much as he could from the accident, Les only rode one horse ever. The very horse that injured him."

Juan joined them, propping his elbow on the gate. "He wasn't supposed to ride any horse. If he'd fallen and hit his head again, he could've ended up paralyzed or dead. Yet he trusted Sam with his life. The horse hurt itself trying not to land on Les when he fell off. That's why he didn't take the full brunt of the blow from Sam's hoof. Les knew Whiskey Sam would take care of him."

"They seem like amazing creatures," Hunter murmured, his attention riveted on Edward.

"So are the horses," Yancey said, a knowing tone to his voice.

Hunter shot a quick glance at the man and Yancey winked at him.

"Edward is at the top of the rider rankings and has been for the past three years. He's done some amazing things with horses of all talent levels. One of the things people like about him is the fact that he doesn't just work with the top-level horses. If a client wants him to and he sees potential, he'll work with horses that might never get beyond the intermediate level. He loves horses, plain and simple. Any breed. Any size. Hell, he even likes ponies and they can be a rough group to deal with." Juan cleared his throat. "I bet he gets her over the fence the first try."

Yancey grabbed Juan's hand then placed a kiss on his knuckles. "I won't take that bet. I've had you win too many of them to risk it."

Edward surprised them all by pulling Dolly up after cantering her for a few minutes. He walked her over to where they stood. "Yancey, can you come in here and check her right front leg?"

"Do you think she's injured? I didn't feel anything when I cleaned out her hooves before I saddled her." Juan's concern showed on his face.

Shaking his head, Edward stroked Dolly's neck while Yancey approached her. "I'm not entirely sure. It's very faint, but it feels like she's favoring that leg. To be honest, I wouldn't be surprised if she turns up lame in the morning."

"Damn. I never would've worked her if I had known."

"Of course not. You aren't abusive to your animals. Like I said, it's a faint hesitation when I ask her to step out on that lead. I think that's why she's been refusing. You've been asking her to take off from that leg and there must be some kind of pain interfering with her doing it. She knows she can't get the power to clear the jump, so she stops."

"Right. When I took her over the poles and the cross-rail, she was on her left lead and didn't have to put as much weight onto the right." Juan rubbed his chin. "I guess I'll cool her down then leave a note for the night guys to keep an eye on her."

Yancey crouched next to the mare, running his hand up and down her leg. He stopped at her forelock and Dolly shifted as though he'd touched something that hurt. "Edward's right. Not sure what it is, but she's sensitive there. Why don't you trailer over to the clinic and I'll do an x-ray? We'll find out if it's serious or just something a little stall rest will fix."

Juan stroked Dolly's nose. "Sounds good to me. I can't believe I missed it."

Edward dismounted then handed the reins to him. "Don't feel bad. I think the only reason I noticed it was because I'm sore on my left side and cautious about doing anything that might actually hurt. She's kind of moving like me right now."

When Juan opened the gate to lead Dolly out, Hunter slid past them to go to Edward. He slid his arm around Edward's waist, encouraging his lover to lean against him. They followed Yancey and Juan into the main barn.

"You can take the smaller trailer since you don't have yours here," Edward offered Juan.

"Thanks, man." Juan stripped Dolly's saddle and bridle off. While he carried them to the tack room, Yancey slipped her halter on then attached the cross ties. "I'll clean her stuff when I get back."

"Don't bother. One of the night shift can do it. Hell, I have a mare about to foal and the birthing crew is on tonight. I was going to tell them to clean the tack anyway." Edward winced when his hip bumped Hunter's. "I think we're going to head back to my place. Give me a call later when you figure out what's wrong. She's still a young horse, so recovery should be quick."

"Take care. Nice to meet you, Hunter." Yancey grabbed a brush then joined Juan in grooming Dolly.

"Nice to meet you as well. I hope everything works out all right." He waited until they were out of earshot of the others before he said, "Maybe you should rethink riding tomorrow if you're this sore after a few minutes on a horse."

Edward huffed, and Hunter couldn't tell if it was an annoyed sound or a pained one. "I'm sore because I haven't ridden in a couple of weeks. I'll stretch tonight and it'll be fine tomorrow. Once I get back into the saddle, the last bit of ache will go away."

He wasn't sure about that, but he had to trust that Edward knew his own body well enough not to do anything to harm himself.

"I've felt worse. Let's wander through the barns at my place then head in for dinner," Edward suggested. "I have some steaks in the fridge we can grill."

"Sounds good to me." He didn't take his arm away though, loving how Edward felt pressed to his side. He paused before they went inside the stallion barn to place a kiss on Edward's lips. "Maybe I could give you a massage after dinner. I bet that would help with the soreness."

Hunter couldn't help but smile at Edward's moan.

"That would be great," Edward agreed then returned the kiss. "I do actually want to take a quick look at the mare. She's been showing signs of going into labor the last day or so. My foaling team is good, but I just want to make sure everything is all set for her."

Even in pain, Edward exuded confidence, and Hunter could see how much the man's employees liked and respected him. The two men who watched over the stallions during the night reported to Edward that everything was good. The horses were bedded down and had finished their evening feeding.

There were four on the foaling team. They showed Edward that all the precautions had been taken. Louisa, the head foaling person, took them to the large birthing stall where the petite bay mare with the huge, extended stomach paced through the thick layer of straw covering the floor.

"She'll give birth tonight. Milk's coming in and she's been pacing like this for the last hour. I can see the contractions have started, but aren't serious yet. Dr. MacCafferty stopped in a little while ago to examine her. As far as he can tell, there shouldn't be any complications. We have his number on speed dial if there are."

Edward chuckled. "Louisa, with as many births as you all have watched over, you could probably handle just about anything that happened."

Louisa was a rather plain woman, but her smile lit up her face and made her beautiful. "True, though it doesn't hurt to have a professional close by in case we encounter something we haven't seen before."

"Did you let her owner know?"

"Yes. He said he'd be out in the morning if everything goes well. Looks like Gypsy will be adding another foal to his list of children. I'll keep my fingers crossed this one turns out like his siblings." Louisa opened the stall door a crack then slipped in. She approached the mare cautiously, making no sudden moves or loud noises. After running her hands over the mare's sides and checking under her tail, she nodded. "I'll have Jenvoski bind her tail to keep it out of the way."

Edward said, "Give me a call if something goes wrong. If

not, I'll see you in the morning."

Louisa waved at them as she shut the stall door then disappeared down the aisle toward the office where the team would wait for the mare to give birth. Edward motioned for Hunter to head toward the house.

"How many offspring does Gypsy have?" Hunter found he was interested in the whole process, though he'd never really thought he would be.

Edward's brow furrowed as though he were counting in his head. "Only about a hundred. He's been at stud for six years. I don't have him cover a lot of mares. A lot of breeders have their studs cover two hundred mares a season. I didn't want that. It's not like I need the stud fees or anything. I want Gypsy to pass on his bloodline and talent, but I don't want to wear him out. He deserves to rest in his old age."

"Two hundred? Wow, that's a lot of horse sex." Hunter snapped his mouth shut and rolled his eyes. "Sorry."

"You're right. What you need to realize is that a lot of planning goes into breeding, especially expensive horses like these. It's not a gentle process and the handlers have to make sure neither animal gets injured. Actually, this mare is foaling pretty late in the year. We usually like to have all the mares foal in the spring. This was a favor for a friend. She's his favorite mare and he's always wanted to breed her to Gypsy." Edward nudged Hunter. "You'll get to see a brand new foal tomorrow morning."

"That'll be cool. Now let's worry about dinner."

He pushed open the door to the mudroom, letting the dogs that had joined them as soon as they got to Edward's farm rush in first before helping Edward inside.

Chapter Eleven

Edward groaned as he sat on the bench then bent over to untie his boots. He let one then the other drop. After wiggling his toes, he contemplated standing up again. Hunter held out his hand.

"I'll help you up. You'll have to show me where the dog food is, so I can feed them." Hunter squinted at him. "Why didn't they follow us over to the training center?"

"I trained them to stay over here once I moved. Some of the horses—and clients—don't like dogs. The ones here don't have a problem with them, so I keep them here. Don't want to upset anyone." Edward reached down to scratch Dudley's ear. "I never understood why people think pitbulls are dangerous. As long as they're trained right, they wouldn't hurt anyone."

Hunter patted Ellie's head before moving into the kitchen. "Unfortunately, not all of them are trained by the right kind of people. Yours are pretty well behaved."

After dropping onto the stool, Edward pointed to a cupboard in the mudroom. "The food is in there and their dishes are in the cabinet next to it. They get two scoops each. Dudley's is blue. While you're doing that, I'll pull the steaks out and go fire up the grill."

"Wait. Do you have any painkillers? Maybe you should take one." Hunter shook his head when Edward started to speak. "Just to take the edge off."

"I have some over-the-counter stuff that'll work." He laughed as Hunter simply stared at him. "There's a bottle in the cupboard next to the sink. If you want to get me two pills and a glass of water, I'll take them."

Hunter did as Edward said before he fed the dogs. After taking the pills, Edward headed out to the veranda, where he got the grill going. He wandered back into the kitchen to see Hunter pulling the steaks out of the fridge.

"There's fixings for a salad and broccoli as a side if you want to make them up." He seasoned the steaks and let them sit for a minute. Propping his hip against the counter, he watched Hunter chop up vegetables and lettuce. After a few minutes, he returned to the grill.

"Here's some iced tea. You probably shouldn't be drinking alcohol right now." Hunter gave him a glass. "The salad's done and the broccoli's steaming. It'll be ready when the steaks are. I'd like mine medium rare, please."

Edward said, "Is there any other way to eat it?"

Sipping the tea, he kept an eye on their food as Hunter wandered to the edge of the veranda to stare out over the large lawn leading to the wooden fences of the paddocks.

"How can you stand to leave this place?" Hunter shot him a glance from over his shoulder. "It's so beautiful and peaceful."

"There are days when it's hard to leave, but then I think about how much I enjoy competing and that I need to make money to keep all of this." Edward took the steaks off, setting them on the plate. They went back inside to the table. Hunter had set it before he'd brought Edward his tea.

After filling their plates, they took a few bites, then Hunter asked, "When did you start riding?"

Edward set his fork down before leaning back in his chair. "I was probably around eight when I got bit by the 'horse' bug. It's weird. You hear about girls and their love of horses, but some guys get it too. Luckily, my father was rich, and while he didn't really care about me one way or the other, he was willing to pay for lessons. It kept me out of his hair."

"Was? Are your parents dead?"

Shaking his head, Edward grimaced. "Well, my mom is. She died in a plane crash with her third husband about four years ago. My dad is still very much alive and traipsing around the world with Derek's mother. He's still rich, but I have little to nothing to do with him anymore. Derek is the only one I care about."

Hunter took a sip of his beer then said, "My parents live down in Florida, having an amazing time in the sun and sand. I go to visit them from time to time. I do know what you mean, though. I have some family that I don't care about seeing ever again."

"I started competing in shows when I was eight and by the time I was seventeen, I knew this was what I wanted to do for the rest of my life. I made a deal with my dad. If he bought me the land and paid to have a barn built, I wouldn't ask for any of kind of inheritance." Edward tapped his knife against his plate. "He had the original training center built on fifteen acres of land. He also bought Gypsy for me. Then washed his hands of me."

"Must be nice to get that kind of start in your job," Hunter teased. "But I guess it was a good investment because you're going strong."

Edward agreed. "I have a gift for riding and understanding horses. They've helped me get over some really hard times."

After standing, Hunter moved around the table to crouch next to Edward. He cradled his head then brought their lips together in a soft kiss. Edward tasted the beer and the steak Hunter had been enjoying. It didn't last long before Hunter broke it off then returned to his seat.

"I can tell that losing Samantha was hard on you," he said.

Staring at his hands, Edward lifted one of his shoulders in a half-hearted shrug. "It was. I mean, I'm not pining for her or anything. I dealt with the grief and moved on, but Samantha was the first time I ever lost someone I truly loved. My parents didn't have a lot to do with me. I was raised by nannies and servants, so when my mom died, I didn't feel anything. She was a stranger to me."

He didn't like talking about his family because he'd discovered most people didn't understand the dynamics. The only ones who did were usually other rich kids who'd grown up much like he had. Les was one of the few exceptions to the lonely rich kid stereotype, since his father had loved him more than his job or his own personal life. Yet people who had grown up with normal lives like Hunter rarely grasped how Edward could be so distant from his own parents.

"How did you meet Samantha again? I know you told me a little in your office." Hunter picked up his silverware, beginning to eat again.

Edward smiled. "I started riding at a different stable because I wanted to work with one of the trainers there. He was a world-class rider and I knew I could learn a lot from him. Samantha took lessons there as well, though she did dressage instead of jumping."

"Dressage? What's that?"

He'd forgotten Hunter hadn't grown up in the horse world. "It's kind of like horse ballet. Elegant balance and controlled power. The horse and rider have a set pattern they have to complete, showcasing each move the horse has been taught. The rider must get his mount to do these certain moves without looking like he's doing it. All his cues have to be so subtle the judges—and the audience— barely notice them." A thought hit him. "I have a Grand Prix-level dressage rider and trainer who uses my barn as her home base. She'll be here tomorrow to work her horses and do some lessons with her clients. If you want, you can watch and see what I'm talking about."

"Cool. I'd like that. Even though I haven't been hanging around you long, I'm finding out that I'm interested in this stuff. I mean, it seems like you're as dedicated to your career as I am to mine. Always practicing to try and get better." Hunter shifted in his chair. "Do you do dressage?"

Shaking his head, Edward chuckled. "I can. In fact, I teach my jumpers lower-level dressage movements. It helps keep them supple and bendy. I don't have the patience to compete. I mean, training a dressage horse takes the same amount of time as training a jumper, but you have to have a certain level of stillness in your soul to be a great dressage rider. I like the speed and explosiveness of jumping."

"Are there other disciplines?" Hunter leaned back in his chair, resting his hands on his stomach as he studied Edward.

"Oh, there are a bunch, but I guess the other major English discipline is eventing. It combines dressage, cross-country and show jumping. It's sometimes called three-day eventing because the competition usually happens over the course of three days. You have to have a very talented horse that is good at all three and fearless, plus a rider that is just as courageous."

Hunter pursed his lips. "What's cross-country? It sounds like some kind of marathon thing."

Edward was impressed. "It sort of is. The rider and horse must complete a course of up to four miles while jumping twenty-four to thirty-six obstacles along the way. All under the time limit set by the event officials. These aren't the kind of fences you see in show jumping. With those, the rails are designed to fall when a horse brushes — or hits — them with his hooves. Cross-country jumps are solid, built not to fall when a horse hits them."

He caught the wince crossing Hunter's face and he nodded. "Yeah. There can be serious injuries on a cross-country course, even deaths. That's why I said eventing horses and riders have to be fearless. Hell, I saw a horse get free of his handlers and race off. As they were chasing him, he actually jumped a smaller SUV, cleared it without hesitation. A great eventing horse will jump anything in his path, which is why they're hard to come by."

While they'd been talking, Edward had managed to clean his plate, then pushed to his feet. Hunter helped him clear the table and rinse the dishes then put them in the dishwasher. They finished cleaning up the kitchen and Edward refilled his glass.

"Let's go into the living room," he suggested. "I can actually show you some videos of both dressage and eventing, if you want. My training facility is multi-discipline. I bought the farm on the other side to add to my land and had a cross-country course built. I've recorded some of the riders doing both, so they can see what they're doing right and wrong."

After grabbing another beer out of the refrigerator, Hunter followed him to the living room where Edward slipped in a DVD of Sasha Jenkins, the Grand Prix-level dressage rider, who trained at his barn. He snatched up the remote before settling onto the couch next to Hunter.

"This is actually at Aachen, Germany. It's one of the most important shows in the world. All the best rider and horse combinations compete. If you win there, you've made it in your profession." Edward pushed play.

"Is it just dressage?" Hunter wiggled until he was pressed close to Edward's side.

"No. There is show jumping and eventing as well. Gypsy and I won the big class three years in a row," Edward bragged. "Two years in a row, Gypsy was the only horse with no faults. He didn't knock a rail down or have a time fault."

Hunter rested his hand on Edward's thigh. "I guess that's pretty good, huh?"

"It is. Not many horses can repeat like that." He fast-forwarded to the point where Sasha entered the ring on her mare, Anna. "Anna was one of Sasha's best horses, but she was injured and Sasha had to retire her. This is one of the highlights of Anna's career."

The music started and Anna began to dance. Or at least it looked like it. He never got tired of watching the top horses doing what they do best. When the program was done, he hit pause and glanced at Hunter.

"Wow. That was amazing. It looked like she was dancing."

"At the Grand Prix level, one of the programs is called Freestyle. The rider can pick a piece of music then coordinate the movements to it. So in many ways, it is a dance." Edward yawned. "You know, that massage is sounding good right about now."

Hunter climbed to his feet then helped Edward up. "Then let's go."

After shutting off the lights and making sure the house was locked up, they wandered down the hallway to Edward's room. Hunter tugged the blankets and sheets down to the foot of the bed while he gathered some towels and a bottle of massage oil he'd been given as a present. He came back to find Hunter sitting on the chair, waiting for him.

"Here." He tossed the oil to Hunter then laid the towels on the bed. Once that was done, he stripped off his clothes, doing his best not to get his shirt hung up on his cast then dropping it on the floor.

Edward crawled onto the mattress before flopping on his stomach. The bed dipped slightly when Hunter joined him. Looking over his shoulder, he watched as Hunter straddled his hips. They exchanged smiles then he rested his forehead on his arms.

The pop of the bottle was the only warning he got before a trickle of cool liquid drizzled across his shoulder blades. *Christ! Glad it's not cold.* He rolled his shoulders as Hunter rubbed his hands over his skin.

He let his eyes drift closed while Hunter worked every muscle in his body. All the tension he didn't even know he carried in his lower back eased. There wasn't anything sexual in Hunter's touch at the moment, instead he seemed intent on helping Edward relax.

"That feels so good," Edward moaned, arching his back a little.

"I was hoping it would," Hunter replied as he edged down to begin massaging Edward's legs.

Edward sighed. "I'd pay you a lot of money just to stay around as my masseuse."

"I appreciate the offer, but you might not want me if we spend too much time together," Hunter joked. "Plus you can afford to hire one to follow you to all the shows."

"That's not a bad idea. I'm not the only one who gets sore

and tense while competing. I'll have to talk to Juan about it." He jolted when Hunter patted his ass. "You're done?"

Rolling his head to the side, he spotted Hunter walking toward the bathroom. He considered getting up, but wasn't sure his legs would hold him. Edward felt as though he'd been liquefied.

Hunter wandered back, holding a glass of water. "Here. You need to drink this before you fall asleep."

He drained it then set it on the nightstand. "I thought you wanted to have sex again tonight."

"Oh, I'd love to, but I can wait. Maybe we'll get some late-night action." Hunter sat beside him. "Though you should probably go wash the oil off before I cover us with the blankets."

"It's all right. If it doesn't come out, I have more sheets," Edward murmured, already finding it hard to keep his eyes open.

Hunter pulled the blankets up over them before curling into Edward's side. Edward fell asleep listening to Hunter hum a slow melody.

Chapter Twelve

Hunter jerked awake when his phone began to play *Smooth Criminal*. He flailed around, fighting with the sheets until he got his arm free so he could snatch the annoying device from the nightstand. He had to rein back his annoyance before he could answer.

"Hey, Boris, what's wrong?" he asked as he pushed himself up to lean against the pillows. He glanced over to where Edward had been sleeping, but that side of the bed was empty. He seemed to remember Edward kissing him at some point and saying something about coming down to the barn when he got up.

"What makes you think there's anything wrong?" Boris' voice was harsh, as though he'd been screaming for an extended period of time.

Hunter rolled his eyes. "Come on, man. You don't call any of us just to chat," he reminded his friend.

"Maybe I'm turning over a new fucking leaf, asshole." Boris grunted then said, "I was just curious to hear how you and Lonnie are doing."

"Why didn't you call Lonnie?"

"Because I don't want to talk to the fucker," Boris stated, then must have decided to clarify. "At least not right now. Figured he'd end joining you wherever you are."

Inhaling deeply, Hunter bit the bullet and asked, "Did you want to join us? We can get a room for you."

To his shock, Boris said, "I think I will. Send me where you're at and I'll come on down. I mean, we're supposed to meet up again next week anyway. Might as well hook up with you early. Maybe we can get some practice in."

"Who are you? And what the hell have you done with Boris?" Hunter was only half-joking. Boris had never cut his vacation short and he'd certainly never considered hanging out with any of them. There were a lot of times Hunter had wondered why Boris played in the band. The man didn't seem like he liked any of them, though he was probably closest to Hunter.

"Shut the fuck up, man. Why can't I just want to hang out with my band members?" Boris coughed.

Hunter didn't like the sound. "Because you never have before. Are you all right? Don't bullshit me, Boris. I want the fucking truth."

The sound that came over the phone was rough and sad. Hunter wasn't sure he'd ever heard anyone make it before.

"I just want to be done, Hunter, with all the shit."

He didn't know what 'shit' Boris meant—whether it was the band or whatever he did while in New York. Yet Boris seemed to be opening up to him for the first time, Hunter wasn't going to turn his back on his friend.

"Then come down here. We still have a week before our next tour. You can crash in the room and rest. You won't have to talk—or see—anyone until we start practicing the new songs." Hunter rubbed his chin. *How am I going to swing this? There's no way I can have Boris and Lonnie share the room. Boris would stab Lonnie with a fork after twenty minutes. Lonnie isn't going to want to stay with Tad the whole time either. Maybe Edward will have a suggestion for another place we can stay.*

"Text me where you are and I'll let you know when I'll be there." Boris was silent for a few seconds before he said, "Thanks, Hunter. I don't know why you put up with my shit, but I do appreciate it, even if I don't show it."

Hunter smiled. He didn't try to help Boris out for the recognition, but he could admit it was nice of Boris to acknowledge what he did once in a while. Hell, it was the first time Boris had said anything about how Hunter held out his hand in friendship.

"You're welcome, Boris. Now get your ass down here.

Text me when you leave New York, so I have an idea when to expect you."

"Will do. Tell Lonnie to pick his shit up. He's probably trashed the room by now." Boris hung up before Hunter could reply.

After texting Boris the name of the B&B they were staying at, Hunter let his phone drop to the sheets beside him. He rested his head back against the headboard and stared up at the ceiling. What the fuck had happened to Boris this trip? It must have been something serious for him to call and ask if he could come stay with Hunter.

Sighing, he scrubbed his hands over his face, deciding to set all those questions aside. He wanted to go find Edward and see the man in his element. Something told Hunter that Edward would be stunning.

When he got out of the shower, there was a pile of clothes sitting on the bathroom counter with a note from Edward.

Washed these earlier for you. E

Thank God he didn't have to put dirty clothes back on, though he'd done it before while they were touring. Couldn't always find time to stop at a laundromat between gigs.

Once he was dressed, he shoved his phone in his pocket then wandered to the kitchen, following the scent of freshly brewed coffee. He smiled when he saw Edward leaning against the island, coffee mug in hand. The dogs sat at Edward's feet, heads tilted as they listened to him talk.

"Silly things. You have to stop trying to play with Scooby. He's a grumpy old goat. He doesn't want to play and he'll stomp your little butts into the ground if you keep bothering him." Edward glanced up when he heard Hunter laugh. "Hey, I'm just trying to impart a little wisdom. I don't want to have to take them to Yancey because Scooby bit one of them — or head-butted them."

"Or kicked one of them. Gypsy doesn't get upset by the

dogs?" Hunter headed right to the pot and the mug Edward must have set out for him.

Edward shrugged. "Not really. I worried at first, because he could be a little high strung in the ring, but he's never reacted to them when they're around him. The milk is in the fridge and sugar's in the cupboard in front of you."

"Thanks." He doctored it the way he liked then took a sip, sighing as the warm liquid filled his stomach. "Coffee truly is the elixir of the gods."

"I've been drinking it since I was fifteen with early morning stable chores then school before going back to the barn for lessons and more chores."

Hunter plopped onto one of the stools by the island. "I thought your father paid for your lessons."

Edward angled to face him. The dogs lay down, resting their heads on their paws. "He paid for a certain amount of them, but if I wanted work with a different trainer for a few weeks—or wanted a new saddle—I had to get a job. I didn't mind. They were notoriously short-handed at a barn, so I could always find someone who would pay me for mucking stalls and cleaning tack."

"Never doubt the determination of a teenager who wants something bad enough, huh?" Hunter grinned. "I wanted a guitar when I was fifteen. My dad told me I had to get a job. He wasn't going to buy it for me. I got a paper route then a job as a bag boy. I didn't enjoy either one, but I saved my money and bought the guitar. Hell, I still have it at my apartment in Richmond."

"I still have the first saddle I bought with my own money. It's kind of beat up and I can't use it on any of my horses. I keep it to remind myself what I can accomplish when I put my mind to it." Edward set his mug down before reaching out to cup Hunter's face in his hands. "Good morning."

Hunter accepted the light kiss Edward gave him. He touched Edward's cheek as the man eased away from him. "Thanks for letting me sleep in."

Edward nodded. "You shouldn't have to get up at five

in the morning if you don't have to. Did you want some breakfast? I came back to put the pie in my refrigerator. Amazingly, no one had eaten it."

"Do you have eggs?" He pushed to his feet. "I can make us scrambled eggs and bacon, if you have any."

"It's all in there." Edward gestured to the refrigerator. "I'll call down to the barn and let them know I'm taking a breakfast break. My first student doesn't arrive until ten, so I have time."

Hunter got the supplies out then set about fixing breakfast for them. He tried not to reflect on how homey the whole situation was. It was far too soon to think about that.

Edward set the table then refilled Hunter's cup.

"Have you heard from Lonnie?" Edward asked while he dished out food for the dogs.

"Dude, it's still morning. Lonnie hasn't even gotten out of bed yet. Well, unless he was in Tad's then he got up, went back to the B&B and is buried under the blankets there." Hunter shook his head. "He's not what you'd call a morning person, which is why I'm not going to give him the news until this evening."

Edward took a spot at the table and Hunter slid some eggs onto his plate. After filling his own plate, he carried it and the bacon over to Edward.

"What news?" Edward took a bite of the eggs and moaned. "These taste amazing. What did you do to them?"

Hunter shrugged. "Mixed in some cheese and spices. It's how my mom makes them. Oh, I got a call from Boris earlier."

Eyeing him, Edward frowned. "Boris? I thought he didn't talk to any of you while he was on vacation."

"Normally he doesn't. I mean, this is the first time he actually reached out and called me on his own. He sounded terrible and wanted to come stay with me until we have to meet up and start practicing for our next tour." Hunter shoved his eggs around his plate while he thought. "I told him to come. I wasn't about to turn him away."

"Of course not. Are you all going to be able to handle being in the same room together?"

Hunter snorted. "That's going to be the problem. If it were just Boris and me, it'd be fine. I've roomed with him before and we get along. But Lonnie puts Boris on edge and I'm pretty sure it would only take about twenty minutes before he drives Boris to murder."

Chuckling, Edward took a couple of bites of his breakfast before he said, "You could just stay at one of my cottages. I think I have one that has three bedrooms. Or…" He paused as though he were nervous about what he was going to say next. "You could stay here with me while Lonnie and Boris take one of the smaller cottages."

"You have cabins? Why?" Hunter's heart skipped a beat at the thought of sharing Edward's bed. He tried to focus on the more important issue of where the others would be staying.

"Sometimes I have visiting riders and trainers. They need some place to stay, so I decided to build some cottages to make it easier for them. It's so they don't have to travel back and forth from town, if they don't want to. Some do choose to stay at Sarah's, but most of them like it here." Edward motioned vaguely at the window. "It's quiet, and while the barn areas are busy, the rest of the farm isn't. Most places the only thing you'll run into is a horse, a dog or a goat. Oh, and a few cows."

"Cows? Do you use them for training?" Hunter smirked.

Edward shook his head. "Not usually. There have been times when I've had cutting horses boarding here for a few friends and they'll ship in their own steers. The cows are from a dairy farm. One of the charities I support rescued them and they needed a place for them to stay. It's not like I don't have the room, so I said they could live here."

"That's nice of you. If you're not careful, you're going to be overrun by animals." Hunter winked when Edward met his gaze.

"Oh, I know. That's how I ended up with those two." He

pointed to the dogs. "Yancey rescued their mother and she was pregnant with them. He needed people to adopt them, so I took two."

Hunter studied Dudley and Ellie. "Makes sense. This way they can play with each other and aren't ever alone."

"Right." Edward took his last bite then sighed. "I have to get back down to the barn."

"No problem. I'll clean up here then come down. Are you at the main training one?"

Edward helped clean off the table before brushing a kiss over Hunter's cheek. "Yes. I appreciate it and I did mean what I said. You're welcome to one of the cabins. None of them are being used right now."

Catching Edward and stopping him, Hunter pressed a hard kiss to the man's lips. "I'll talk to Lonnie and Boris about it. It'll be the perfect solution. I think Boris really needs some place he can hide out for a little while."

"Like I said, no one will bother him." Edward hugged Hunter then strolled to the back door. "Come on, you two. You can run around outside for a while."

Dudley and Ellie dashed out of the door in front of Edward. When he was alone in the kitchen, Hunter dropped into the chair, propping his chin on his hand and his elbow on the table. How had he gotten so lucky in meeting Edward? He must have been doing something right and the universe had decided to smile down on him. Like he'd said, Edward's offer was the perfect solution. If Lonnie decided he didn't want to stay out at the farm, he could have the room at the B&B. Hunter and Boris would use one of the cottages.

He pushed to his feet, quickly rinsing the plates and silverware before putting them in the dishwasher. He got it running then put his boots and jacket on. Shoving the door open, he stepped out onto the back porch and took a deep breath. The cool, fresh air filled his lungs. It was an experience he didn't have often, since most of the time he was in a city, where the air was tainted with gas fumes and other pollutants.

Hunter chuckled when he saw a foal wobble over to his mother then head-butt her side. "Little thing must be hungry," he murmured. "I wonder how the mare did last night."

Detouring to the foaling barn, he walked as quietly as he could down the aisle toward the mare's stall. He'd almost gotten there when Louisa slid open the door then stepped out. She saw him and grinned.

"Did she have it?" he asked, eager for some reason.

"Yes. A beautiful little colt." She gestured for him to come closer. "They'll stay inside for a couple of days while we keep an eye on them. Once he and his momma get the all clear from Dr. MacCafferty, we'll let them out with the other families."

The dark brown colt stood on shaking stick legs, his overly large head almost unbalancing him. His mother watched, standing close but not interfering in his cautious efforts to walk. The baby entranced Hunter and he leaned against the wooden wall to watch the colt explore his new world.

Louisa touched his shoulder. "They're so cute when they're brand new. It's what I love most about my job."

"I can see why." He moved away. "I'd better head down to the main barn, or else I'll be spending the entire day here."

"You're always welcome to come back and check on him. The more he gets used to people being around, the better he'll take to being handled by them." Louisa clapped him on the shoulder then walked away.

Chapter Thirteen

"Rachel, you need to sit still on him as you approach the jump. Any unnecessary movement is going to put him off his stride and he'll either leave early or refuse," Edward told the young lady riding Excalibur, a big chestnut Thoroughbred cross, in a circle at the end of the arena.

He stood in the middle of the pattern of jumps he'd set up for them to try. The pair had been together for only a month and while he thought it was a good pairing, it was going to take more time for them to learn how to trust each other. The gelding had a lot of scope and willingness. He'd take her to the higher levels once they had a couple of shows under their belts.

As Rachel brought him into line for the first jump, Edward spotted movement at the window of the family viewing area. He glanced over to see Hunter standing there. He nodded to acknowledge Hunter's wave then turned his attention back to Rachel.

This time she sat chilly, a term Edward had heard used to describe jockeys sitting on their mounts during a race. He watched as she steadied Cal, the horse, then made a soft kissing noise. They'd come in at just the right amount of strides and Cal propelled them into the air. He stretched out over the jump, receiving enough rein from Rachel so he didn't feel constricted as he landed.

She shot Edward a glance and he motioned for her to continue. He'd set up six jumps at different heights and widths with different stride counts between them. He wanted to see just how much Rachel knew and how much she would trust Cal to do. She was a new student. He'd taken her training over from Jeb Carmichael, another top rider, who'd had a bad wreck a couple months ago and was still recovering.

They cleared all the jumps with Cal putting in some extra power at the last one and clearing it by a foot. Edward laughed and Rachel's smile lit her face.

"You can let him walk now," he said as he checked his watch. "Our time's up, but you can take him out on the trails to spend some more time with him. He can be trusted out there without another rider, though I'm sure you could find someone else to go with you if you want." There was always someone around who wouldn't say no to a trail ride.

"If you're sure he'll be okay, Mr. Monterrose, I'd love to go for a hack with him." Rachel scratched along Cal's mane. "I'm so glad you and Mr. Carmichael recommended my dad buy him."

"When I saw Excalibur, he'd just come off the track, but I have a friend who retrains racehorses for other disciplines. We both thought he had what it took to be a jumper. Jeb never had any doubt he'd be perfect for you once he got some training in him." Edward patted Cal on the nose as the gelding reached out to sniff him. "Now go on and relax. Get to know each other, but don't forget to make sure he's cooled down. He got a good workout today."

"Yes, sir." Rachel paused by the gate then dismounted. Edward had a rule about riders not being mounted in the barn area. Most riders had better control of their horses when their own feet were on the ground.

They strolled through the barn area and Edward saw Talon tacking up his mare. "Hey, Talon, are you here for a lesson?"

The young man looked up then shook his head. "No, sir. Just thought I'd exercise Wilbur here. He's a bit of a pig and if I don't give him regular rides, he'll plump up. Carrying extra weight isn't a good thing on the cross-country course."

"True. Would you be willing to let Rachel join you? She's kind of new here, and I want her to take Cal out." He saw the way Talon's eyes widened when he spotted Rachel and hid his smile at Talon's eager nod.

"Sure. No problem. I'll be happy to show you around, Rachel. Wilbur's good with other horses. Actually he prefers to hack with others," Talon babbled.

Edward checked his watch again. "Good. You can show her which trails are safe this time of year and which ones to avoid because of hunting season. I'll see you in two days, Rachel."

"Yes, Mr. Monterrose," she said distractedly, studying Talon with interest.

He walked in the direction of the family area, happy with himself.

"Playing matchmaker, huh?" Hunter spoke from where he sat on the couch facing the arena window.

"Not necessarily. Rachel's new. She moved down from New York to train with me while her own trainer is recovering from an injury. It's hard when you're sixteen and moving around to follow a dream." He sat next to Hunter, resting his hand on the man's thigh. "Having a friend can make things easier."

Hunter shifted closer, leaning against him. "She moved down here to train? What about her family?"

"Her mom came with her, but her dad stayed in New York because of his job. He works on Wall Street, which is why they can afford to let Rachel do this. Of course, not all of my students are as lucky as she is. Some work here to pay for lessons and borrow horses." Edward watched as one of his stable hands began to dismantle the jumps in the arena.

"That's nice of you," Hunter commented. "Giving those less fortunate a chance."

Edward shrugged. "They just don't have the money. It doesn't necessarily make them less fortunate. It gives me free labor, plus I can foster a few dreams along the way. Majority of them never go beyond amateur status. Yet I know they're just as happy with that as I am when I win a big class." He squeezed Hunter's knee before standing. "I have a break in between lessons. I can take you back into town now, or you'll have to wait until around three before I get another one."

Hunter smiled. "I don't mind hanging here if it's all right with you. I spotted the guitar in your office at your place. If I get bored watching the lessons, I'll just go back there and work on some songs until you can head out."

"Fine with me." Edward bent down, kissing Hunter before stepping away. "The next lesson is outside. There are a few bleachers along one end of the arena. You can sit there. It's not too cold yet."

"Will the rider be upset that I'm watching?" He followed Edward out of the room. "I don't want to make them uncomfortable."

Edward motioned to a tall woman standing next to her stallion. "Martha, you ready? We're going to be in the outdoor ring today."

She nodded then led her horse outside.

He turned to look at Hunter. "She's competed in front of audiences before. If having you there throws her off her game, then she's going to have work harder."

Hunter looked skeptical, but Martha spoke up. "Edward's right. I've been riding for a lot of years. If having someone watch me, even as good looking as you are, bothers me, I need to go back to basics and figure out why. And Krew here" — she patted the stallion's shoulder — "is about as bombproof as a stallion can get. You're not going to bother him."

"All right. If you both say it'll be fine, I'll believe you." He went to the stands at the other end of the arena.

"One thing. If you have your phone, can you put it on silent or vibrate? That would be the only issue we'd have," Edward called.

Hunter waved his hand to show he'd heard him. Edward opened the gate for Martha to walk through. Krew swished his tail, but didn't show any interest in him.

"You know the drill. Mount up then walk him around the arena on a loose rein. Do that a couple times then check your girth." Edward motioned to two stable hands standing nearby. "Let's get the jumps set up."

He kept an eye on Martha while he showed his helpers where to place the jumps and what height to make them. Krew was an experienced jumper and had proved he could clear five-six fences without a problem. Edward wasn't sure he had the power to go higher and Martha was more than happy to stay at that height. Hell, they'd been cleaning up at the amateur shows in the area.

Martha walked the stallion around the ring twice then brought him into the middle where she moved her leg forward to check the girth. Edward taught all of his students to double check the girth before they did anything faster than a walk. Sometimes it wasn't as tight as it should be and trying to jump with a loose saddle could cause a lot of problems.

By the time she'd finished that, Edward had the jumps up at the height and place he wanted them. He walked over to Martha.

"All right. You have a total of ten jumps. Various heights and widths. Also, there are various stride counts between them. I've noticed that both you and Krew have been getting a little lazy during your classes. You're letting your form slip. Nothing bad has happened so far, and luckily you aren't in a hunter — or equitation — class, but if we don't nip it in the bud, it could get worse."

She grimaced. "You're right. It's more my fault than Krew's. I haven't corrected him when I saw he wasn't doing it right. Like you said, I got lazy and figured as long as we got over the fence, the style didn't matter."

Edward moved back into the center where he could see her entire ride. "In a way, you're right. But if you let him get lazy about this, what else might he try? He's a smart horse. While he is pretty bombproof for a stallion, he's going to test you to see what you'll let him get away with."

Martha didn't reply, just cantered Krew around the jumps to get an idea of the layout then she headed for the first jump. They cleared it without any problem, but as they came into the second one, Edward could see the horse was rushing the fence.

"Ease him back a little, Martha. He's rushing. We don't want him taking off too close," Edward shouted.

She tightened the reins slightly, forcing him to slow down. It was a thin line between backing him down too much so he wouldn't have any momentum to jump and easing him just enough. He figured Martha would know exactly the point where Krew would begin listening to her again.

They cleared the wall and continued on. During the next hour, Edward commented and showed Martha where Krew had grown lazy with his jumping. Also, the stallion wasn't listening to her as closely as he used to. By the time they'd finished, both Martha and Krew were sweating.

Edward gestured for her to come to him. "Lesson's done for today. Make sure you cool him down all the way before you put him back. If you can, tomorrow, take him out on the trails. See about reconnecting with him. I'll see you in two days and we'll go over everything again."

Removing her helmet, she shook out her hair then settled the helmet back on. That was another rule in Edward's barn—no one rode without a helmet. He'd seen more people saved because of those than he wanted to think about. Not too many of his clients argued with him.

He opened the gate, letting Martha and Krew out. The jumps could stay up, since he knew Juan had a couple of students who needed to work over higher fences. His next lesson was a teenager just getting into jumping. Brendan had been riding since he was seven, but had just decided that show jumping was where his interest lay.

Edward had taken the kid on as favor to Scout, who was Brendan's cousin or something. Scout swore he had a knack for riding, but Edward would be the judge of that. Though if Brendan was anywhere near as talented as Scout, the kid could end up being a top rider in the sport.

The bleachers were empty when he looked over at them and Edward smiled. He hadn't expected Hunter to last as long as he had. The guy had left when there'd only been about five minutes left in Martha's lesson. Edward hoped he hadn't been too bored.

After walking up to the main barn, Edward spotted Scout and a skinny kid in jeans and a Henley standing near the entrance. Scout had his arm around the kid's shoulders, whispering intently to him.

"You'd better not be telling him lies about me, Scout," Edward said as he approached.

Both guys jumped then twisted around to face him. The kid's face was red as though he'd been caught doing something bad. Scout just rolled his eyes.

"I was telling him you were an annoying know-it-all who would torture him every way that you could, but in the end, you'd make him into a damn good rider," Scout replied before shaking Edward's hand. "Glad to see you resuming your usual routine. Got up on a horse yet?"

"Not one of my own. I rode Dolly, Juan's new mare, last night." He snapped his fingers. "That reminds me, I need to check with Juan about her. He was trailering her over to the clinic to get x-rays done last night."

Scout blinked. "She get injured? When I left, she was looking good, though I could see Juan was having trouble with her."

Edward grimaced. "She seemed off in her right front when I rode her. I told Juan about it and Yancey told him to bring her over for a check-up. I haven't seen Juan yet to ask him how that went. He should be here soon. He has a lesson then I know he was going work some of his own horses."

"Cool. I have to talk to him about a class we're both in next month. He's been at this show before and I want to know what to expect." Scout clapped the kid on the shoulder. "Brendan, this is Edward Monterrose. He'll be the biggest pain in your ass, but he's the best trainer you could ever hope for."

Brendan swallowed loud enough for them to hear him then held out a shaking hand. "Thank you for taking me on, sir."

After shaking his hand, Edward shrugged. "I'm happy to do Scout a favor. He said you'll be using one of his horses. Which one?"

"He's letting me borrow Bertram's Buckle. Said that Bertie's getting older and could use an easy life now." Brendan rolled his helmet around his fingers. "My mom can't afford a horse for me."

"Bertie's been one of Scout's best horses for several years, but he's right. While some would say Bertie should be retired, Scout and I talked about it. Bertie's getting slower, but he's not ready to be put out to pasture. What you're going to be learning right now is perfect for him. He'll still feel useful and you'll be riding a horse that can teach you something." Edward took hold of Brendan's arm. "Let's get you saddled up and start this lesson."

Chapter Fourteen

Hunter looked up from where he sat on the floor in the living room. The dogs had deserted him a few minutes ago when the back door opened. He figured Edward was there to take him back to town. Hunter admitted to himself that he didn't want to go back—he kind of liked staying at Edward's.

The house had been quiet and without any distractions for Hunter to get lost in. It made composing the music for his songs easy. The papers beside his knee were filled with music notes and words to be put into lyrics later.

Edward stood in the doorway, holding both arms above him with his fingers clinging to the door frame. His shirt had ridden up, exposing a thin strip of tanned skin as he stretched. Hunter leered and appreciated the view.

"I hope you weren't too bored today," Edward said, moving into the living room then flopping onto the couch. His knee bumped Hunter's shoulder.

"Hell no. I got a new song written along with some bits and pieces of others that I'll need to fine tune into something." Hunter wrapped his hand around Edward's ankle. "Being out here seems to agree with me."

"Well, like I said, you're welcome to stay with me. We can go get your stuff from Sarah's. Also, you can tell Lonnie he's welcome too. I know you'll probably want to talk to Boris about one of the cabins, but there's room for you all." Edward leaned forward to run his fingers through Hunter's hair. "I like listening to you play. I heard you while I was taking off my boots."

Ducking his head, Hunter said, "Thanks. It's the one thing

I found I'm really good at."

Edward winked. "You're good at a few other things." He jumped to his feet. "Did you want to eat here or grab something in town?"

Hunter blinked at the quick change of subject, but decided to let it go. "We can eat in town. I'll text Lonnie and see if he wants to meet us at the café."

"Actually there's a nice steakhouse just outside of town in the opposite direction from the B&B. He could meet us there, or we can pick him up." Edward looked down at his clothes. "Let me go change. I can't go anywhere smelling like the south end of a north facing mule."

"What?" Hunter burst out laughing. "Where the hell did you hear that?"

Edward seemed proud of himself. "I heard it from an old race horse trainer I met years ago. I always thought it was funny."

"It's freaking hilarious, man, but you're right. You might put people off their food if you went in smelling like that." Hunter flapped his hands at Edward. "Go change. I'll pick up my crap."

He kept chuckling softly as he gathered the papers and pens along with Derek's guitar. After returning the instrument to its place and the pens to the desk in Edward's office, Hunter folded the papers before stuffing them in his jacket pocket. *I've got to get a small notebook that I can carry around with me. It'd be so much easier than trying to find paper then hoping I don't lose any of them before I can transfer them to my journal.*

His bigger notebook was with his stuff in their room. He could get his own guitar as well. Rubbing his palms on his jeans, Hunter fought the urge to pace. It was silly really. Why was he nervous about crashing at Edward's for a few days? It wasn't like he was moving in. He was just staying there to help Boris out, whether they all ended up on Edward's farm or Boris stayed at the B&B.

He nearly jumped out of his pants when his phone buzzed.

After tugging it from his back pocket, he checked the caller ID before he answered. "Hey, you're alive. I thought maybe Tad had you tied to his bed and wasn't going to let you go."

"Fuck me," Lonnie growled.

"Shit. You don't sound good. Are you coming down with something? Or are you just now getting back to the room?" Either one was a possibility with Lonnie.

"I'm just waking up. I see you didn't make it home last night. Was he any good?"

Hunter sniffed then remarked, "I don't kiss and tell, asshole. Hey, are you hungry? Edward is bringing me back and said there's a good steakhouse on the other side of town. You could either meet us there or we can pick you up on the way by."

"Pick me up," Lonnie replied right before he hung up.

"Grumpy bastard," Hunter muttered, holding his phone and staring out of the kitchen window.

"I assume you're talking about Lonnie," Edward commented as he walked by on his way to the mudroom.

"Yeah. I guess he just woke up. Said he wanted us to pick him up on the way to the steakhouse." Hunter laced up his hiking boots. "He gets an attitude if he doesn't sleep enough."

Edward slipped into a pair of tennis shoes before grabbing a wool jacket from the coat rack. "I know how he feels. It's hell getting old. There used to be a time when I could stay up all night then go out and ride four classes in a row. Winning most of them too. Now if I don't get at least six hours of sleep, I'm a bigger asshole than I usually am until I've had about five cups of coffee."

He understood what Edward was saying. Even when he got enough sleep, Hunter never felt human until he had his first jolt of caffeine for the day. Edward led the way to a dark green Chevy Silverado crew cab truck. It had Highland Farms painted on the doors. It wasn't the vehicle Hunter thought Edward would drive.

"This is nice," he complimented, running his hands over

the leather seat.

"Thanks." Edward gave him a knowing look. "But you didn't think I'd drive a truck."

Holding up his hands, he said, "Guilty as charged. I guess I saw you driving some kind of European sports car. Maybe it's what I think goes hand in hand with the way you carry yourself."

After turning the vehicle on but before he put it in drive, Edward glanced at him. "I carry myself like I'd drive some kind of expensive vehicle?"

"When I met you, I could tell you came from money. It was just the set of your shoulders. The clothes you wear. Kind of the whole package says you've got money." He put his fingers on Edward's lips to stop him from saying anything. "Don't get me wrong. I'm not saying you come off arrogant or self-righteous. You don't. It's obvious you're a relatively normal guy who just happens not to have to worry about anything."

He cringed because he got the feeling he was explaining it all wrong. Edward grabbed hold of his hand then pressed a kiss to his fingertips.

"I think I know what you mean. I can't help the way I carry myself. A lot of it comes from riding. Keep your back straight and your shoulders back. It becomes second nature, even when I'm not on a horse." Edward let go of Hunter's hand before backing the truck up. "I do have an obscenely expensive Ferrari, but I rarely drive it. My father bought it for me when I turned sixteen. I don't know why he thought giving a sixteen year old a car like that was a good idea. I would've rather he got me a new horse. It sits in my garage most of the time. Oh, I take it out once or twice a year to blow the dust off, but it doesn't have a lot of miles on it."

A Ferrari? Edward owned a Ferrari that he just let sit in his garage. Hunter couldn't believe it.

"I suppose you and your friends could take it for a spin if you wanted." Edward pulled out onto the road. "A truck is more useful to me. I haul horses all over the East Coast and a sports car isn't really built to pull a trailer."

Hunter could feel his mouth hanging open as he stared at Edward. "You'd really trust me and the guys with your car?"

Edward put his knuckle under Hunter's chin and nudged his mouth closed. "Why not? It's just a car and it's fully insured. If you wreck it, it's covered."

"Fuck. See what I mean about having money? The thought of us doing something to it really doesn't freak you out?"

"No. Now I wouldn't put any of you up on my horses without making damn sure you knew how to ride." Edward slowed down while passing a horse and rider on the side of the road. He waved at them as they went by. "Of course, my horses are far more important to me than any piece of metal—no matter how expensive it is. Hell, half of my horses are worth more than that car."

Hunter couldn't wrap his mind around Edward's nonchalant attitude toward the car and the thought that some of the horses he'd seen were worth more than the Ferrari. It boggled his mind.

Edward patted his arm. "Don't think on it too hard, Hunter. The horses don't know how much they're worth. Well, most of them don't. I think the mares have a pretty good idea and they act like queens at times."

He didn't know what to say, so he stayed silent for the rest of the drive to the B&B. When they arrived, he jumped out. "I'll go get Lonnie. Hopefully he didn't fall back asleep."

"I'll go chat with Sarah. See how the reservations are going. Some of the guests stay here so they don't have to drive home afterward."

Edward split off to head back toward the kitchen area where they could hear Sarah chatting with someone. Hunter dashed up the stairs then down the hallway to his room. He almost fell flat on his face in his haste to open the door.

Lonnie raised his eyebrows at Hunter's rather inelegant entrance. "Having a klutzy moment?"

"Edward has a Ferrari and he said we could drive it," he

blurted and fell into the chair.

"Really? He must be touched in the head to let us anywhere near the thing." Lonnie snickered. "He's never seen any of us drive."

"Hey, I'm a great driver," Hunter protested.

"Do you watch Judge Wapner as well?" Lonnie dodged when Hunter tossed a pillow at him. "I was just asking. Did you leave Edward down in his vehicle just so you could race up here and tell me about the car?"

Hunter remembered the other reason they were there aside from picking Lonnie up. "No. He's talking to Sarah about his benefit. I'm going to be staying with him while we're in town."

"Called me shocked at that revelation," Lonnie snarked. "I'm not too upset at getting this room all to myself."

While packing his bag and making sure he had his song notebook, Hunter filled Lonnie in on the conversation he had with Boris. "So you see, you can share this room with Boris or share a cottage out at Edward's place. The choice is up to you and Boris. Personally, I think you'd do much better in the cottage. More space and you'd each have a room to yourself. That way Boris won't be forced to injure you in some way."

"I'm not that bad. Is it my fault the prick can't take a joke?" Lonnie pouted when Hunter pinned him with a knowing look. "All right. He makes an easy target. If he weren't so fucking serious all the time, I wouldn't be compelled to fuck with him. He should just smile once in a while. Instead he acts like it would hurt him to enjoy life."

Lonnie's description of Boris was accurate, yet Hunter had seen the man smile and laugh. There was happiness in him, but it was buried deep under whatever burdens Boris carried.

"Whatever. Pack your shit. You might as well go out there tonight with me. I'll let Boris know about the change of plans. He hasn't gotten back to me about whether or not he's left New York." Hunter dug out his phone then sent

Boris a text.

Lonnie threw all his stuff in his bag and they went downstairs to check out. Sarah wasn't upset about them leaving earlier than they'd planned.

"There's a tour group coming in a day or two and I'll be able to offer them more rooms this way." She surprised them both by hugging them. "It was wonderful to meet you both and I'm sure I'll see you around town. Also at Edward's party, right?"

"Yes, Sarah. They're going to be part of the entertainment," Edward told her, wandering in from the kitchen holding a half-eaten cinnamon roll.

Hunter frowned. "I thought we were eating at the steakhouse."

Edward grunted. "I couldn't resist. Here, have the rest." He handed over the roll then hugged Sarah. "I'll call you next week with the final number of rooms I'll need."

"Great."

Lonnie glared at Hunter, who after one bite had decided he wasn't going to share with his friend. Edward shook his head at their squabbling. They tossed their stuff in the back, and Lonnie climbed in the crew cab as well.

When they were on the road, Edward met Lonnie's gaze in the rear view mirror. "I see Hunter convinced you to take me up on the offer of the cottage."

"Yeah. He had a point about Boris and me sharing a room. It's not a good idea. Separate bedrooms are a great idea." Lonnie curled his upper lip. "Boris takes himself too seriously."

"And you don't take most things seriously enough, Lonnie. You shouldn't harass him because he's different than you," Hunter admonished.

Lonnie wrinkled his nose. "Who are you? My kindergarten teacher? If he can't take the teasing, he needs to grow some balls."

Hunter reached into the back seat and smacked Lonnie on the knee. "You need to grow up too. We're not teenagers anymore."

"Whatever," Lonnie muttered. He turned his gaze out of the window. "It'll be different to have a nice place to stay. Usually on our tours, we're in kind of crappy motels."

"We're not that big of a band. A CD or two and a song on the radio once in a while doesn't make us stadium-level performers," Hunter pointed out. "We make enough to support ourselves, and really that should be enough, right? We're doing what we love."

A grunt from Lonnie was all he received in reply. Edward shot him a wink before turning the truck into a parking lot. The restaurant was in a mock-plantation house and the wait staff was dressed like any would be in a fine dining establishment. Hunter glanced down at his jeans and boots.

"Are you sure we're dressed all right?" He motioned to Lonnie and himself when he asked Edward.

"You're fine." Edward smiled at the little blonde hostess. "Jessica, can I get a table for three? I don't have a reservation, but since it's early, I thought we might be in luck."

Her pretty face lit up when Edward spoke and she nodded. "There's always a table for you, Mr. Monterrose. Follow me."

Jessica led them on a winding path through the main restaurant area. The table she took them to was in the corner. They could see anyone who might approach them. After they sat, he looked at Edward.

"Are you usually put in the corner?" He picked up the menu Jessica had set in front of him. "Sort of like getting a time out because you've been bad?"

"Not that bad. I gave the chef some start-up money to get the place going, so now he makes sure there's always a table open for me. It's not the same one each time." Edward didn't even bother opening his menu. "Order whatever you'd like. It's on me."

Lonnie's eyes widened and Hunter snorted.

"You should've never said that. He can eat."

Edward waved his hand, dismissing Hunter's comments.

"Don't worry. Eat whatever you want. We'll stop at the grocery store on our way back to the farm. You can get food and stuff for your cottage. I called my housekeeper. She's cleaning the cabin closest to my place for Lonnie and Boris."

"Speaking of which, have you heard from him yet?" Lonnie nudged Hunter with his foot.

"No. I sent him Edward's address, so hopefully he'll figure out to go there instead of the B&B. If he hasn't changed his mind and decided to stay in the city." Hunter hoped Boris was on his way to Virginia. Something in Boris' voice made Hunter think that if Boris stayed in New York, he might not come home again.

Chapter Fifteen

When they returned to the farm, Edward escorted Lonnie and Hunter to the Blue Cottage. It was the biggest one, and the closest to Edward's home. It had three bedrooms and a lovely little kitchen. He'd stayed there while his own place was being built.

"Pick whichever bedroom you want. Two have queen-size beds and the third has two twins." He began putting the groceries away while Lonnie and Hunter wandered around the place.

"This place is awesome."

He smiled at Lonnie's comment. His housekeeper had done a marvelous job. All the surfaces sparkled and she must have had help to wash all the plates, cutlery and glasses. It had been at least six months since this particular cottage had been used.

"Man, there's enough room, we could get Andey and Scott to come and we can practice for the next tour here," Lonnie spoke as they walked back into the kitchen. "I mean, they have the van and the instruments. There's room in the garage for us to set it up."

"Umm...maybe you should ask Edward if it's all right with him before you start making plans like that," Hunter suggested. "Remember, this is his place and he might not want the noise upsetting the horses."

"The horses aren't that close. When I bought this place, I knocked down all the old barns and moved them back away from the house and cottages. I didn't want them upset by people coming and going. So any music you played wouldn't bother them, though it might annoy the humans," he joked.

Hunter moved to stand in Edward's personal space, staring up at him. "Do you mean it? When you offered, I didn't plan on taking over like this."

He touched Hunter's cheek. "You're not taking over anything. I'm offering. Why make things more difficult for you when your friends can all gather here before you leave?"

After nuzzling Edward's hand, Hunter stepped back. "I'm thinking our tour might be quite a bit smaller than Derek's."

Edward shrugged. "In a way, yes, but Derek's not doing stadiums this time. He's doing small venues. An intimate evening with Derek St. Martin, is how it's being billed. Just him and his guitar. He said he's always wanted to do something like this, and after his last tour, he's worn out. Max, his husband, forced him to take an extended vacation then convinced him it was the right time for acoustic concerts."

From the moment he'd met Max, he'd known the rancher was the right guy for Derek. He kept Derek grounded and didn't allow him to overwork himself anymore. They were a good couple.

"Cool. I'll call Andey and Scott. Tell them to get their asses down here by the weekend. That'll give us all of next week to practice some new songs and figure out a new play list. I want it to be half covers and half original stuff." Lonnie tugged his phone out then strolled out, mumbling to himself.

"I have to get back to the barn. I don't have any more clients today, but I need to get back on my horses. I have a couple of shows the week after and I want to be ready to ride in them." He took a kiss from Hunter before leaving.

It would've been too easy to stay in the bright kitchen, chatting with Hunter about everyday things. Unfortunately, Edward had horses to work, as well as getting rid of his own stiffness. He needed to test his arm and collarbone, see how much pain he'd be in while he rode. If he knew, then he could prepare for it during the classes.

"I'll have dinner ready around six at your place," Hunter called. "Let me know if you're going to be later."

"All right."

He meandered back to the main training barn where he found Juan leaning against Dolly's stall door. His friend was frowning and Edward knew Juan probably hadn't gotten good news the night before.

"Hey, Juan. I meant to find you and ask earlier, but what did Yancey discover about Dolly?" Edward inquired as he joined Juan.

"She seems to have some kind of infection in her forelock. There isn't a cut or anything there, so I'm not sure how it happened. Yancey says she'll need antibiotics and stall rest for at least a month." Juan scratched his chin. "I'm sending her out to Uncle Tony's ranch. They'll keep an eye on her, make sure she gets the medicine she needs while keeping her in shape. That way she's not taking up a stall in your barn without earning her keep."

Resting his elbows on the top of the wall, he studied the mare. "You know I don't care about that. You're more than welcome to keep her here."

Juan shook his head. "Thanks, but I already made arrangements. Les is sending a plane for her. That way she doesn't have to stand in a trailer for the time it'll take to drive out to Wyoming. Besides, I have a new horse I want to try out. He's arriving on Friday and can take her stall."

"Replacing Dolly already?" Edward stroked the mare's nose as she sniffed him.

"Of course not. She's going to be a good jumper once she heals from this, but I have an owner who wants me to try out a gelding of his. He bought it from a guy in Germany, swears he has top-shelf bloodlines."

Edward rolled his eyes. "Doesn't matter how blue their blood is. If a horse doesn't want to jump, it won't."

Juan eyed him. "I know that, which is why I told him I'd

try the horse out. If I think he has potential, I'll add him to my string. If not, I'll send him back to his owner and tell him to find something else for the gelding to do."

Dolly lipped Edward's fingers and he tapped her on the nose. "None of that, girl. Just wait until you get to Tony's. You're going to be spoiled beyond belief. Not just the guys at the ranch, but Les and Randy will be over, visiting as well. Les can't resist a well-bred horse."

"I figure I'll be getting a call from him within an hour of his seeing her. He'll be asking me how much I want for her. I'm tempted to let him buy her, but keep riding her for him. It's not like I don't have a few of his in my string already." Juan shifted to face Edward. "You taking Salt for ride?"

Nodding, he thought about the horses Les had sent him over the years. Most didn't own all the horses they rode. They might train, board and ship them to shows, but other people owned the animals. It helped up-and-coming riders get good mounts without having to spend a lot of their own money.

"Want me to hang around while you ride? Just in case," Juan offered.

"Thanks. I know you've been exercising him for me, but even with regular riding, he can be a handful." Edward went to Salt's stall then took his halter off the hook on the door.

"Don't you have any you can start back riding on that aren't as high strung?" Juan unlatched it then slid it open enough for Edward to slip in.

Salt nuzzled his chest before sniffing his hair. Edward got the halter on him then led him to the crossties. Juan brought Salt's grooming box and tack, setting them down out of the way. Edward picked some hay out of the stallion's mane.

"You are a silly beast," he whispered. "Never staying clean for long. I swear if I put you out in the paddocks, you'd be covered with mud from head to tail."

Juan laughed. "Jewels was the same way. I think he loved being brushed, so he took advantage of every mud puddle he could find. My grooms despaired of ever keeping him clean."

They worked in comfortable silence as they groomed then tacked Salt up. Walking over to the indoor arena, Edward took some deep breaths. There was always a pit of nervousness in his stomach the first ride after a fall whereas normally, he was able to get right back on and didn't have to think about broken bones.

He nodded his thanks when Juan brought over the mounting block. He didn't need to prove anything to himself—or Juan—by mounting Salt from the ground. Once he was on, he let Salt walk around on a loose rein while he readjusted to being back in the saddle.

Juan stayed by the gate, but called, "Did you want me to set up a few jumps? I'll make them small. It might help get the rust out."

"Sounds good."

Salt paused and Edward could almost guess the horse was wondering if he should spook at the paper fluttering in the corner of the arena. Edward nudged him.

"Keep going, Salt. You don't need to be afraid of that. It won't hurt you," he encouraged the horse.

Snorting and shaking his head, Salt walked on as though he'd never once considered freaking out. Edward knew better. While Salt was a professional in the show ring, he was a bit of a clown and nervous nelly in the practice arena. He'd have to keep an eye on the stallion to make sure he didn't do anything to hurt either of them again.

"I set up four. One stand alone. A three-fence combination with two strides going into the first. One stride between A and B then two strides between B and C. The B fence is wide, so he'll have to jump big." Juan moved to the middle of the arena. "Too bad I didn't have time to set up a liverpool. We'd get a chance to see if Les' training stuck this time."

"I'm glad you didn't," Edward admitted. "I'd like one ride under my belt before I take him over a water jump, though Scout said he had him go over a couple of them the other day and Salt didn't blink an eye at them."

Juan sniffed. "Of course he didn't. The horse is an idiot. Best damn jumper I've seen in a long time, but so flighty sometimes."

"Which is why I won't sell him. It would take a long time for a new rider to become familiar with his quirks. Plus, as annoying as he can be sometimes, I'm fond of him." Edward patted Salt on the shoulder before gathering the reins. He urged the stallion to canter as they circled the arena. He got a look at the pattern Juan had set up for him and also let Salt get a peek at them, just so he knew they were there.

He wiggled the bit in Salt's mouth, making sure he had the horse's attention, then aimed him toward the first fence. It was a simple four-foot wall made of foam bricks. If Salt hit one with his hoof, it would fall. It was the type of fence Salt tended to get careless going over. The stallion knew the bricks weren't real and he didn't always tuck his legs under as much as he should.

But this time Salt leaped over it without any issue. Maybe he was behaving because Edward was on him, or maybe he just wasn't interested in acting up right then. They headed into the combination and Edward could see how tight the stride was between A and B. He collected Salt then asked him.

They landed, took one short stride then jumped, with Salt stretching out to make it over the entire width. There was no hesitation when they landed. Salt listened to Edward, took the two strides he'd asked for before jumping the last fence. As they galloped out from the other side, Edward winced at the twinge of pain in his wrist.

"You both looked good," Juan told him as he cantered Salt past him. "Go through it in the opposite direction then I think you're good for the day. You know what to expect from your injuries. Your schedule is light tomorrow, right?"

Edward nodded.

"Then you can ride a couple of your other horses tomorrow. Get the younger ones used to you again," Juan suggested. "I know you have someone waiting for you back at your place, so don't waste any more time here tonight. I'll make sure everything's put away and the horses are bedded down."

"What's Yancey doing? I thought he wasn't supposed to be working," Edward asked.

Juan frowned. "He isn't working, technically. He's having dinner with a couple of the other vets in the area. They meet once a month to update one another on what's going on in their neck of the woods. It helps them keep track of things. Making sure they don't have an outbreak of something — or if they do, they can catch it in time before it gets too bad."

"Sound plan." Edward turned his focus back to the jumps and how Salt was acting.

They cleared all four without incident, though Salt did rub one of the bricks. Since it didn't come down, Edward decided to let it go for the night. He'd have to figure out something to fix the problem, but that was for another day.

He cooled Salt down then brushed him out. After putting a blanket on him, Edward took him back to his stall, where one of the stable hands had already put his feed and a bucket of water. Juan caught Edward as he was leaving Salt's stall.

"Here are the files from today. Everyone's opinions on their students and horses. I'll see you in the morning. Tell Hunter I said hi." Juan handed him a stack of folders.

"Thanks. Be careful driving home." He tucked the folders under his arm before meandering back toward his house. He'd go over them tonight then have one of his assistants enter the data into the computer.

Dudley and Ellie greeted him when he strolled through the gate that separated his breeding farm and home acreage from the training facility. They danced around his feet while he walked over to the foaling barn.

"Good evening," he greeted Louisa as he entered.

She hugged him. "You look tired."

"I just took Salt over some fences in the arena. Testing my wrist to see how it goes." He went with her to Starla's stall.

"How's our newest addition?"

"He's doing really well. His owner was here this morning and was happy to see them both looking good. I figure by Friday, if Dr. MacCafferty gives the okay, I'll put them out in the paddock with the other mothers and foals." Louisa checked the colt out with Edward.

The colt stared at them for a second then tried to race around the stall. Unfortunately, he wasn't coordinated enough on his spindly legs, so he fell over before he got a foot away. His mother sniffed him to make sure he was okay then nudged his hip, encouraging him to get back up.

"He's bigger than her last one," he remarked, tracing the lines of the colt's back and chest.

"Oh yeah. He's going to be a big boy when he's fully grown. Makes you wonder what he'll end up doing. Might be a good eventer. He certainly has the bloodlines for it."

Louisa was right. His dam, Princess Starla, had competed at the four-star level until her owner had retired her. While Gypsy had been better at jumping, his own bloodlines ran heavy in eventing horses as well.

"Could be." Edward squeezed her shoulder. "You should go home. Give the rest of your team a chance to lose some sleep tonight."

"I think that's a fabulous suggestion. I'll see you tomorrow."

"Yes, ma'am."

He continued through to the stallion barn where he checked on them and the night shift. Once that was taken care of, he went up to his house. Walking through the door, he took a deep breath and his mouth began to water. Something smelled delicious. He rubbed the dogs' ears then removed his boots. He hung up his coat before padding into the kitchen.

Chapter Sixteen

"God, it smells good in here."

Hunter straightened from where he'd been bent over to get the casserole out of the oven. He turned to grin at Edward. "I hope it does, since it's dinner."

Edward swooped in to kiss him, avoiding the hot dish in Hunter's hands. "Do I have time to change and wash up a bit?"

"Yes. The casserole has to sit for a few minutes. What do you want to drink?"

"Iced tea. I'm going to take a couple of muscle relaxers. My shoulder and wrist are bothering me." Edward disappeared down the hall.

"Of course they're bothering you," Hunter muttered, shaking his head as he set the dish on the table. "It's not like you're completely healed."

He finished setting the table and filling the glasses before Edward wandered back in, wearing a pair of sweatpants, a faded T-shirt and socks. Hunter wouldn't have believed Edward owned a pair of sweats if he hadn't seen them right then.

Edward sat then reached for the salad. "What did you and Lonnie do after I left you?"

"We started going through our old playlist, trying to decide which songs we want to keep and which ones we want to change. We'll come up with about forty then when the others get here, we'll narrow it down to about twenty." He scooped out some of the casserole onto Edward's plate. "Do you know how long Derek's going to want us to play before his set?"

"Have no clue. He and Max will be here middle of next week. You can talk with him then about the performance." Edward grimaced. "Next week is going to be crazy. All the final preparations for the benefit. Making sure there are enough tables and chairs. All the food."

Hunter eyed him. "You don't do it all yourself, right? You have assistants to help you."

Edward cleared his throat. "Oh hell yes, I have assistants. JoLynn and Katy are in charge of it, but I have to give approval on the big stuff before it gets ordered. Also, I go over everything with them the day of to make sure we have everything. There have been times when something hasn't shown up, but then we just wing it."

"In addition to a full schedule of students and training rides, right?" Hunter was exhausted just thinking about all the work Edward did every day. Hunter assumed there were a lot of things Edward had to do himself.

"Yes. The horses don't care what's going on at the barns. Hell, all they know is there's a lot more people and trucks coming and going. More noise and distractions for them." Edward took a bite of the main dish and moaned. "This is amazing. How'd you learn to cook like this?"

Hunter's cheek warmed and he ducked his head slightly at the praise. "My mom wanted to make sure I knew how to cook some meals while I was on the road. She didn't want me eating at fast food places all the time."

"I hear moms are like that," Edward remarked. "My parents' cook did teach me a few simple things, then I took some cooking lessons. Mostly so I could impress the people I was dating." He leered at Hunter, who laughed.

"Are women as impressed by a man who cooks as men are?" Hunter wondered. He didn't have a lot of close female friends. Being on the road the majority of the year put a damper on friendships.

Edward shrugged. "I don't know if they're more impressed or not, but I do know they appreciate not having to cook all the time. And a romantic dinner to surprise them always helps. The guys as well."

What is it like being attracted to both men and women? Hunter wasn't sure he had the nerve to ask because it really wasn't any of his business. Maybe after they got to know each other better.

"Did you ever date girls?" Edward questioned as he added some more vegetables to his plate.

"No. I knew I didn't like girls that way by the time I was twelve. I didn't know it had a particular name. It was just how I was." Hunter finished his meal then sat back in his chair. "What about you? I mean, it's obvious you date women. When did you know you liked both?"

Edward squinted at the wall across from him as he seemed to be thinking. "I was around sixteen, I think. It was around that time I realized I wanted to kiss William as much as I did Rhonda. I was shocked at first, but then I got used to it. The dating pool is wide open for me."

"True." He sucked it up and asked, "What's it like being attracted to both? Was it as difficult for you growing up as it was for a gay kid like me?"

Tilting his head, Edward replied, "I don't think so. Being attracted to women made it easy for me to blend in more when I was younger. Especially if I was in a place where I knew liking guys could get me into trouble. Nowadays, I don't have to worry about it. Mostly because I don't care what people think. I've had a few serious relationships with women, Samantha being my first. A few serious ones with men. Unfortunately, none of them lasted."

Hunter stood then gathered his plate. Carrying it to the sink, he said, "Why didn't they last? And if you don't mind me asking, do you see yourself settling down with a man or a woman?"

Edward joined him at the sink. "Some of them didn't last because I was young and not interested in settling down—as in getting married kind of settling down. Others ended because I travel frequently for my job, plus the horses take up a lot of my time when I am home. The people I was dating couldn't handle not seeing me that often, I guess."

Hunter understood that part of it. Whenever he had a relationship end, it was usually because his significant other thought he cared about his music more than he did them. He wouldn't say they were wrong — music had always been the one thing he was good at when he was younger, then it had became the one constant in his life, along with the other guys in the band.

"As for getting married?" Edward paused for a second then continued, "I guess I never really put a face to the picture of the person I would marry. I don't care if they're male or female. That's not important to me. I want someone who loves me and who can deal with the horses. They don't have to love them, though that would be a bonus. They'd just have to accept the fact that for right now, I'll be spending more of my time in the barn than the house." He took hold of Hunter's arm then pulled him close. "What about you?"

Hunter lifted his chin to meet Edward's gaze. "I've never thought about it either. Mostly because I'm still trying to figure out my music career. Will we ever make it big or will we just be a traveling band up and down the East Coast? It's not a bad way to make a living, but it's hell on relationships. None of us ever had one that lasted longer than six months, I think. It'd take a special man to fall in love with me."

"It seems we're searching for the same thing," Edward whispered against his lips then kissed him deep and hard.

Luckily Hunter had already set his plate down in the sink or else there would have been pieces of broken dish all over the floor. He slid his arms around Edward's waist then slipped his fingers under his sweats to grab his ass. Opening his mouth, he allowed Edward to sweep inside.

While he sucked on Edward's tongue, he trailed his fingers along the man's crease, rubbing over his hole. Edward jumped but didn't stop kissing him. Hunter grunted when his back hit the counter. Easing a few inches away, he met Edward's desire-glazed eyes.

"We should move this to the bedroom. Cleaning up can wait," he murmured then took Edward's hand to lead him to the bedroom.

Edward didn't protest, just followed him as closely as he could. When they stood next to the bed, Hunter cradled Edward's face in his hands. "Let's try something different this time. I want to feel you inside me."

"I'm all for that," Edward said softly. "The lube and condoms are on the nightstand. How should we do this, since I can't put pressure on my wrist?"

"Get naked then lie on the bed. I'm going to ride you." He tugged on the hem of Edward's shirt and Edward took the hint.

Stepping back, Hunter watched for a minute while Edward stripped off his clothes. He had to admit that riding kept Edward in amazing shape. Muscular thighs. A tight ass. Washboard abs. He reached out to trace the lightly furred line bisecting Edward's stomach to his groin. Hunter encircled the base of Edward's cock then stroked up to squeeze the flared head.

Edward let his head drop back as he moaned. Hunter continued to tease and play, rubbing his thumb over the pre-cum-slicked flesh. He lifted his thumb to his mouth then licked it clean. After placing his other hand on Edward's chest, he gave him a slight push.

"All right," Edward said, chuckling as he fell. "I get the point, but you need to have fewer clothes on to do this."

"I'll get right on that." Hunter bent to wrap his lips around Edward's shaft and sucked, letting his flavor coat his tongue.

Edward buried his fingers in his hair then pull gently. After lifting his head and letting Edward slip out of his mouth, Hunter straightened before quickly disrobing. He tossed his clothes in every direction, not caring where they landed.

"Get in the middle of the mattress," he ordered while reaching for the lube and rubber Edward had left out.

Once he made sure Edward was where he wanted him, Hunter crawled onto the bed then straddled the man's hips. He tossed the foil packet on Edward's chest.

"Get this on," he demanded. "I'll get myself ready."

"But I wanted to do that," Edward protested.

"Maybe later we can take the time to play," Hunter said. "I need you in me as soon as possible."

Edward didn't argue after that. He struggled with the foil packet because of his cast, but he managed to get it open. He rolled it on then held out his hand. "Give me some lube."

Hunter popped open the bottle then squirted some into Edward's palm. He then covered his fingers before reaching behind him to rub them over his own opening. Not interested in taking it slowly, he shoved his fingers in to stretch and get his channel ready for Edward's cock.

Bracing his hand on the sheets beside Edward's head, Hunter arched his back then rocked, impaling himself. He worked as fast and as hard as he could, but paused when Edward grabbed his arm.

"It's time," Edward said, gripping Hunter's hip with his other hand. "I want to be in you when you come, Hunter."

He removed his fingers then took hold of Edward's length. He positioned himself over it then slowly lowered himself. Edward held him at the waist, giving him support to balance as he bounced up and down. Hunter angled his hips just right so that each time he went down, Edward's cock nailed his gland.

The pressure built until he almost couldn't stand it. He needed something more to get over the edge. He went to take a hold of his own shaft, but Edward slapped his hand away.

"I've got this," he told him.

Undulating between Edward's grip and his shaft, Hunter couldn't stop until his climax burst over him, spilling onto Edward's hand and stomach. He cried out as his inner muscles clamped down around the flesh inside him.

"Hunter," Edward yelled, slamming deep then flooding

141

the condom.

As much as Hunter tried, he couldn't stop from collapsing onto Edward. He whimpered as Edward embraced him and they shuddered together in the last moments of their climaxes. Sweat and cum held them together while they tried to calm their hearts.

When he was sure his muscles had got their strength back, Hunter rolled to one side, wincing as Edward slid out. He ran his hand through the mess on his stomach and grimaced.

"We should probably take a shower then go clean up the kitchen," he suggested.

"Sounds like a good idea," Edward agreed then climbed off the bed before shuffling toward the bathroom.

Hunter followed close behind. He helped wrap Edward's cast in a plastic bag as the water warmed up. Once that and the condom had been dealt with, they got in the shower and washed quickly.

Edward slammed his elbow against the tile wall and swore. "This is always so awkward," he muttered.

"I could've taken one after you," Hunter said.

"What? No." Edward shook his head. "I don't mean you being in here with me. The shower is definitely big enough for the two of us. I mean doing shit like washing up with a bag on my arm. I've broken both of them so many times you'd think I would be used to this by now."

Hunter cringed. "Have you ever broken them both at the same time?"

Edward rested against the wall for a moment. "No. Thank God."

They washed the soap away, then Hunter got out first before offering to help Edward dry off. After that, they dressed then went to the kitchen. Hunter refused Edward's assistance, telling him to sit on the couch and go over the files he'd brought home.

As he finished putting the last glass into the dishwasher, his phone rang. It was Boris. He snatched it up from the counter then answered, "Where the hell are you, man?"

"Halfway to you. Why?" Boris sounded better than he had the last time they'd talked.

"You didn't text me to let me know when you were leaving. Then I sent you the address of the new place we're staying and you didn't get back to me about that either." He sometimes felt like he was dealing with a teenager when he talked to Boris.

"Huh," Boris grunted. "Sorry, dude. I just wanted to bail out of the city fast and must have forgot about calling you. But I'm doing it now. I'm all right and I should be to you by midmorning tomorrow."

Hunter considered that. "Be careful. Don't drive too fast. If you get tired, stop and sleep. You don't have to be here by any specific time."

"I'm not tired, but if I do stop, I'll call you." What sounded like a car door slamming came over the phone. "I'm back in the car, so I gotta go. I'll see you in the morning."

"All right."

Boris hung up without saying goodbye and Hunter sighed. At some point, they were going to have to figure out what to do about him. But it didn't have to be tonight. He had a gorgeous man to cuddle with while watching TV.

Chapter Seventeen

Knocking on the door caught Hunter's attention and he poked Lonnie in the side.

"Go answer that," he ordered. "I want to work this chord out."

Lonnie grumbled, but did as Hunter told him while Hunter stayed bent over his guitar, plucking out a chord that just sounded off. He needed to figure out why.

"Look what the cat dragged in," Lonnie said as he walked back into the living room.

Hunter set his guitar aside when Boris came in a few steps behind Lonnie. He hugged the man tightly, ignoring how stiff Boris was in his embrace. Boris was never one for hugs or a casual arm around the shoulders. He didn't like his personal space invaded, but Hunter often chose to ignore that. And of course, he was the only one Boris let get away with it.

"Good to see you, dude. How was the drive down?" Hunter motioned to the furniture. "Pick a seat. Did you want something to drink or eat?"

Boris' pale skin emphasized the dark circles under his green eyes. The haunted and hunted expression was there — the one Hunter always noticed when Boris came back from New York. There was a slight hesitation as Boris sat, almost as though he were in pain, but Hunter ignored that as well. Questioning Boris the instant he arrived was the surest way to get the man to leave.

"Drive was fine. Not too many cops out, so I made good time." Boris coughed. "I wouldn't mind some iced tea, if you have any."

Lonnie didn't even wait for Hunter to say anything. "I'll get it for you. You want a refill as well, Hunter?

"Yes." Hunter returned to his spot on the floor. "We'll give you the tour of the place and show you your room after you've relaxed for a little while."

Boris waved his hand around, encompassing the room. "This is a nice place. Never picked you or Lonnie as horse people, though."

Hunter smirked. "I'm not really a horse person, but I am partial to a certain man who rides horses."

"So that's how it is," Boris said, giving him a knowing look. "You're a good enough lay that he'll give you a cottage to vacation in, huh?"

"It's not like that," Hunter protested. "I just made a comment about you wanting to come down here and that I hoped the B&B had another room open. I know you and Lonnie can't share a room without killing each other. Edward said he had these cottages that were for visitors and we could use one if we wanted."

"Where are you sleeping?" Boris leaned back against the couch cushions and crossed his arms.

Blushing, Hunter dropped his gaze to his notebook. "I'll be staying with Edward."

"Uh-huh."

"Shut the fuck up, Boris." Lonnie stalked in, practically shoving Boris' glass in his face. "It isn't any of your business what Hunter's doing and how we got this place. Edward's a nice guy and he's not doing it just because Hunter's sleeping with him. Get your head out of your ass."

Hunter took the glass Lonnie held out to him then met Boris' gaze. His friend almost looked ashamed, which was strange because Hunter didn't think Boris ever felt guilty about anything.

"Sorry," Boris mumbled.

"Never mind. Just try not to be a jerk when you meet Edward. He's really giving us a chance. You know who Derek St. Martin is, right?"

145

Boris nodded.

"He'll be at this benefit we're playing at in a little over a week. If he likes us, we might get a shot at a record deal — or at least another audition for one."

Their last deal had fallen through after they'd recorded one album for them. The marketing hadn't been there for their CD to be a success. Hunter chalked it up to experience and had written down what they'd do differently the next time they got the chance.

"I'll believe that when I see it," Boris commented, but he did smile. "Hey, why not give it a shot? It could end up being a good thing. I mean, look, we already got a great place to practice for the next week."

"Yeah. Andey and Scott will be here on Friday with the instruments. By then, we should have some new songs, plus an idea of what covers we want to add to the playlist. Also, St. Martin arrives the middle of next week and he'll let us know how long he'd like our opening set to be." Hunter picked up his notebook then tossed it at Boris. "I've written a couple of new songs. Check them out. You'll need to write in the keyboard parts."

Boris paged through the notebook until he found the ones Hunter had marked. Lonnie sat next to him and they started talking over the melody. The only time those two really got along was when they were working on music together.

Hunter plucked out another melody that had been dancing around his head for a day or two. It was slow and he had the feeling the words would be more of a love song. He was uncomfortable about playing it for the others, especially now, after Boris' reaction to coming here.

"That's pretty," Lonnie spoke up from where he sat. "Is it done?"

Hunter wrinkled his nose. "Not yet. It'll take a while. Not sure if I like it that much anyway."

"Oh no." Boris ripped out a piece of paper, crumpled it up then threw it at him, hitting him in the nose. "You finish it. As much as I hate agreeing with jackass here, I think it's pretty. It might be one of your best, but you'll never know unless you get it written."

"Since when do you give pep speeches?" Lonnie stared at Boris as though he didn't know who the man was.

Boris smacked him upside the head. "Shut up. I'm just telling him to keep going. Of course, it could suck, which to be honest, it probably will because it's a love song, and everyone knows those don't mean shit."

Sighing, Hunter rolled his eyes. "There's the Boris we know and love. I'll finish it, but I'm not sure I'll show it to either of you now."

His phone vibrated before either of his friends could reply. He saw it was Edward, so he stood then walked out of the room. "Hey there, why are you calling me when you're just at the barn?"

"I thought I'd make sure everything was going all right. I saw your friend arrive. He talked to Katy and she gave him directions to the cottage. Did he find you?" Edward sneezed. "Sorry. Helping throw down some hay for the stalls."

"What? Should you be doing that with your arm in a cast?" Hunter couldn't believe anyone would be stupid enough to allow Edward to do that.

"Umm...I'm going to take the Fifth on that one," Edward hedged. "We could take your friends out for dinner tonight. Let Boris see the town and everything."

Hunter shook his head. He should've known Edward would push as far as he could. "Are you sure you want to put up with Lonnie and Boris together? Separately, they're a handful. When they're together, they can be more like little kids instead of adults."

Edward coughed, though it sounded like he was trying not to laugh. "I don't have a problem. If they act up, we'll sit them at other tables while we enjoy our meal."

"I should've thought of that. I might have to do that when we're on tour. When did you plan on quitting for the night?"

The silence in the other room unnerved him, so he peered around the wall to see Boris staring out of the window overlooking one of the paddocks. Lonnie still sat on the couch, scribbling in Hunter's notebook. *At least they aren't killing each other quietly.* He leaned back against the wall.

"Probably around six. I'll have to come back to the barn when we return to go over the scheduling. We have to register for upcoming shows and I need to see which horses and rider pairs will be ready for which class. Then I talk to the other trainers about their students." Edward sighed. "We'll have a lunch meeting sometime next week and make the decisions. My assistants will get the forms filled out and the money paid."

"Sounds complicated."

"Not so much complicated as time-consuming," Edward told him. "Have to make sure the horses and riders get to the right classes so they can earn points for other shows."

Hunter didn't understand what Edward was talking about and he was pretty sure it wasn't something he'd ever need to figure out. "Okay. Then I'll see you around six."

"Great. Have fun until then."

After hanging up, Hunter wandered back into the living room. Boris glanced at him from over his shoulder. "Done talking to the boyfriend?"

He wasn't interested in arguing with Boris about Edward. "Yes. He's going to stop by here at six and we're going out to dinner. That way you can meet him. Try to be polite for the first hour or so."

Boris raised his eyebrow. "The first hour? Wouldn't you want me to be on my best behavior until you can hook him?"

"I think he's already hooked, though it's only been a few days, so I can't tell for sure," Lonnie spoke up. "We'll know for sure when we go out on tour. If he still sticks around after Hunter's been gone for three months, I'd say it's for real."

"What about Hunter sticking with him when he goes to

shows?" Boris saw Hunter's look of surprise. "What? I know a thing or two about the horse world, and your boyfriend is going to be gone just as much as you are. Trying to keep a relationship going with just phone calls and text messages can be difficult. Depends on if you want it enough."

Hunter had time to make the decision. He wasn't going anywhere for a couple of weeks and as far as he knew, neither was Edward. They'd talk about their relationship when the time came to leave. He wasn't going to push it any faster than necessary.

"He seriously wants to go out to dinner with us?" Lonnie squinted. "Is he trying to gain favor with us? We are kind of the only family you have around here."

"Ugh! You two. He wants to meet my friends because he hopes you'll like him. Just like any new boyfriend. Haven't either of you ever wanted to meet a guy's family and friends after you've been dating for a while?" Hunter settled on the floor in a huff.

"Well, no," Boris admitted. "I don't date men. I fuck them and leave. One-night stands, that's all. More than that and it gets complicated."

Lonnie jumped to his feet then raced over to punch Boris in the shoulder. "I agree with him on that. Though my reasoning is usually I'm just passing through. I don't hook up with someone while I'm home on vacation. Don't have an excuse to leave then."

Boris shoved him away. "What kind of operation does Edward run here? I saw the horses and all those people at the main building, but didn't get a good enough look to figure out what they were doing."

"He shows and trains jumpers. Plus he teaches lessons for people who want to learn. He's one of the best in the world. There are also other trainers who board their horses here. They do other disciplines as well. Eventing and dressage."

He noticed that Boris did seem to be listening to him, which was odd since Hunter didn't think Boris would be interested in horses or the people who rode them. "I can't really describe what the other two are. It's very complicated, but I'm sure if you want to know, Edward would be happy to tell you. If you stay out of the way, you could probably watch some of the riders train."

"I might do that," Boris said. "I like animals. I assume the dogs that greeted me are Edward's as well."

"Yes. He's trained them to stay on the land the breeding farm is on. That way they don't bother the clients' horses. From what I can tell, the horses here don't mind the dogs wandering around, though it sounds like the goat hates them." He smiled at the thought of Scooby chasing the dogs off.

Lonnie whooped. "Scooby! I want to see that silly goat and that pony...what did Edward call him? Lollipop? They were cute."

Hunter stared at his friends. He never would've thought either of them would enjoy hanging at a farm for a day — much less a week.

"All right. Boris, let's get your bags from your car and toss them in your room. After that, we can tour the farm. As long as we don't bother the horses, I'm sure it'll be all right." He hoped it would be okay. *Guess if it's not, someone will stop us.*

Boris threw his bags in the other room with the queen-size bed then joined Hunter and Lonnie outside on the small front porch of the cottage. Dudley and Ellie sat with them, tails wagging as the men petted them.

"Let's go."

They wandered around the breeding farm for an hour. They laughed at the antics of the foals in their paddocks and even helped lead the mares when it was time for them to come inside for the evening.

Louisa taught them how to groom the horses. Boris truly seemed in his element, taking to the job without fuss or very much instruction. Lonnie was far more interested in playing with Scooby and Lollipop. Hunter found he enjoyed the rather soothing repetitiveness of brushing a horse. It was obvious the horses had no complaints about how long it took them to finish up.

"Well, if you boys decide to make a career change, let me know. I could always use good grooms like you," Louisa joked as they led their respective animals into their stalls. She was the one in charge of the foals since the men didn't have the first idea how to lead a youngster.

By the time they made their way back to the cottage, Edward was sitting on the porch steps, playing fetch with the dogs. When he stood, Hunter walked right up to him before kissing him. He didn't feel the need to hide in front of Lonnie and Boris. It wouldn't have been the first time they saw him kiss a man.

After the kiss ended, Edward took a step back. "Why don't you go wash up a little? Don't worry about your clothes. There's a diner just down the road we can go to. They're used to horse people coming in at all hours of the day and night."

"Good, because we're starving and I don't think any of us want to take long enough to clean up enough to go to the steakhouse," Hunter said as Boris and Lonnie joined them. "Boris McKenzie, this is Edward Monterrose. Edward, this is my friend and the keyboardist for our band, Boris."

"It's good to meet you. I'm glad you were able to join Hunter and Lonnie early." Edward shook Boris' hand.

"Thank you for letting us crash here. You have a marvelous facility." Boris' tone was very polite and respectful.

Hunter hoped it was a sign of how the rest of the time they were at the farm would go.

Chapter Eighteen

"Have we hit the big time or something?" Scott commented as he strolled into the cottage where Hunter, Lonnie and Boris were having lunch. "Got a fancy place to practice and work on new material."

After standing, Hunter hugged his friends then gestured to the stove. "There's mac 'n' cheese, if you want something to eat. We also have stuff for sandwiches."

"How was the drive?" Lonnie asked while the other two were getting food.

"Not bad, but we only stopped for gas. I'm starving." Andey piled meat on his sandwich.

Once they were all seated at the table again, Scott eyed Hunter and said, "Lonnie says you hooked up with the guy who owns this place."

I won't blush. I won't blush. Hunter's mantra didn't work. His cheeks warmed. "And so what if I am?"

"Lonnie says it might be serious," Andey continued the interrogation.

"Lonnie fucking talks too much," Boris muttered, leaning over to punch Lonnie in the arm.

Hunter laughed as Lonnie tried to dodge Boris, but ended up falling out of his chair onto the floor. "It does seem like he's talking about stuff he shouldn't, but he might be right about it being serious. I'm not sure yet because it's only been a week or so."

Scott shrugged. "I'm not entirely convinced time matters when you're falling in love. Hell, I met Matt and knew I loved him within minutes. It's the staying in love where time is important."

They all stared at him. Hunter hadn't realized Scott had had a serious relationship with anyone. He wasn't as secretive as Boris, but he also wasn't out picking people up like Lonnie.

"Are we ever going to meet Matt?" Hunter thought maybe he could get their attention off his love life.

"He was in the military and deployed a lot, which is why you never met him." Scott fidgeted with his silverware. "He's not re-enlisting this time around, so you'll probably meet him sooner than I really planned."

Studying his friend, Hunter said, "Is that why you said time is more important in staying in love? Because you've had to deal with being without him for months?"

Scott nodded. "Yeah. I think it's going to be a harder adjustment having him around more than it was realizing I loved him."

"Did you invite him to the benefit? I'm sure Edward wouldn't mind adding him to the guest list," Hunter inquired.

"No. He's still trying to decide where he's going to live. Right now, he's out in California since that's where he was based when he was in the military. He's thinking about coming to Arlington, or maybe going to Austin where his brother lives." Scott pointed at them with his fork. "When you do meet him, I expect you all to be on your best behavior."

Lonnie pressed his hand to his chest. "I'm hurt you think we wouldn't give the moment the respect it deserves."

Andey flicked a noodle at Lonnie. "Shut up. We know you're the one who'll act like an asshole. Boris will just ignore him and Hunter knows how to act like an adult."

"Notice he said you know how to act like one. He didn't say you were one," Boris pointed out to Hunter.

"Acting's fine with me," Hunter mumbled then stood, somehow managing to catch the piece of bread Lonnie launched at Andey. "All right, you two. We need to clean up then get the instruments set up. Maybe get a jam session in to get rid of the rust, huh?"

The others jumped to their feet and hurried to do what he suggested. While they sometimes fought and argued, they'd become brothers in every way except blood as they chased their dream of becoming stars. They were serious about their music.

Within an hour, they were playing some of their favorite covers. The garage door was open and Hunter could see people coming and going from the different barns. Every once in a while, they'd pause as though they were listening to the band. He hoped the noise wasn't too loud. None of the horses out in the paddocks seemed bothered.

Glancing around, he noticed three black and white cows standing in the paddock closest to their cottage. They were pressed against the fence, faces turning in his direction. He burst out laughing and stopped playing. The rest of the band stopped as he kept giggling.

"What the hell? We were on a roll, asshole." Lonnie stalked over to kick his foot. "Why'd you stop? What the hell is so funny?"

"We have an audience. They must love your voice." He pointed at the cows.

Andey, Scott and Boris all joined in the mirth once they saw the animals. Lonnie looked annoyed. Hunter wasn't sure if it was because of his teasing or because he'd stopped playing. At times, Lonnie could be a diva.

"They appreciate a great voice when they hear one," Lonnie said, lifting his chin before whirling around. "Let's do that one again and try to ignore the bovine critics."

"Ooh...Lonnie knows big words," Scott mocked.

After flipping him the bird, Lonnie grabbed his microphone. "Come on, guys. Let's get this done, then we can start working on some of the new stuff Hunter's written. It's good."

He wouldn't say that, but once everyone had added their part to the melodies and helped tweak the lyrics, the songs would work. It was one of the things he enjoyed about working with the guys. Separately, they were all good at what they did, but together, they were great...at least in his opinion. Hopefully other people would think the same thing and sign them to a record deal that would actually pan out this time.

Losing track of time was standard when they played. It wasn't until Hunter's hands started to cramp that he checked the clock. "Fuck! Okay, guys. We need to take a break."

Scott groaned as he straightened from where he'd sat hunched over his drums. "Probably a good idea."

"Why don't we grab some water, then I'll take you on a tour of the farm? You'll know where you can be and where you need to ask before you go." Hunter set his guitar aside. "Remember, don't touch any of the horses without permission. Edward doesn't own all of them and the owners might not like strangers touching them."

"I'd like to see them," Andey said. "My dad used to take me to the track. He was friends with a trainer and I'd get to watch the racehorses train. It was pretty exciting. Does your guy have any Thoroughbreds?"

Hunter shrugged as they made their way inside for water. "He might. I've never asked him the breeds. I do know the benefit we're playing for is to support a couple different nonprofit charities. They take Thoroughbreds that are retired from the track and re-train them for different disciplines instead of them being sent to auctions where they might be sold to slaughterhouses."

The guys looked suitably appalled by the thought, just like Hunter had been when Edward had explained what happened to some of the horses no one wanted. He was happy to know he was playing for a good cause.

After getting drinks, Hunter led them out to the paddocks where the mares and weanlings were segregated. There were only two mares with young foals and they were in a paddock, so the youngsters could play together. The other mares grazed without hurry on the grass. Their stomachs were starting to get distended as their babies grew inside.

"These are weanlings, meaning they no longer drink their mothers' milk. They won't be considered yearlings until January first." Hunter let one of them nibble at his sleeve for a second before gently tugging it out of his mouth.

"Why?" Boris smiled as the herd took off as though they'd heard a starter's gun. They raced around the paddock, bucking and jumping as they went.

"Just something they do with horses. No matter what time of the year they're born, their birthday is January first. I guess it helps make keeping track of things easier."

Hunter gestured to the mares in the next paddock over. "Most of them will give birth in the spring."

Andey grinned. "You probably never thought you'd learn so much about horses in your life, did you?"

Shaking his head, he admitted, "No, I didn't, but I'm fascinated by it all. The animals are beautiful."

"They are," Scott agreed. "Let's go see some more."

They wandered around the farm and training facility, doing their best to stay out of the riders' way. Hunter took a quick look in Edward's office. Finding it empty, he wondered if he was riding or teaching a lesson.

"Hey, Hunter, you looking for Edward?" Juan approached them, leading a tall, bright chestnut horse.

"I wanted to introduce him to the rest of the band. Andey and Scott, this is Juan Romanos. He's one of the trainers here." He motioned to his friends.

"Nice to meet you." Juan nodded at them. "Edward's in the arena. He's riding Salt and going to help me evaluate this guy."

Disappointment raced through him. "Oh, I don't want to bother him then. We can catch him later after he's done."

"Why don't you come and watch? I don't mind and I know he won't," Juan told him.

He glanced at the others, who nodded and agreed. "All right."

"Great." Juan walked in front of them and Hunter thought

he heard Andey sigh.

Then Andey leaned into him, whispering in his ear, "I'd follow that ass anywhere."

Hunter could admit Juan had a nice ass, but he thought Edward's was better. "He's married, so don't touch."

"Damn," Andey muttered, but winked at Hunter as they walked into the family area. "This is cool."

He turned his attention to the man in the arena. Edward looked magnificent on Salt—they truly moved as though they were one. Salt shook his head and Edward laughed. Then Juan and his mount appeared.

"Is that Edward?" Scott asked as he joined him by the window.

"Yes. You'll meet him later tonight. We're having dinner for everyone at his house." Hunter raised his hand when Edward glanced over after Juan spoke to him.

"Wow." Scott sounded stunned. "That man loves you, Hunter. No doubt about it. I can see it in his eyes."

Hunter huffed out a laugh. "You're just seeing things."

Scott took a hold of his arm when he would've turned away from him. "Listen. I don't talk about my love life that much. Mostly because once I met Matt, I've been off the market—so to speak. But I do know what love looks like. The look on his face is the one I see every time Matt looks at me. You're going to have to make some decisions soon, man."

"Decisions?" He was glad the others couldn't overhear them.

"About how hard you want to make your relationship work. I gather he travels as much, if not more, than we do. Love's rough when you're both on the road all the time." Scott frowned. "I'm an expert on that."

Staring at Edward as the man rode Salt around the edge of the arena, Hunter thought about Scott's words. As much as he protested about it being too soon to know how he felt about Edward, Hunter knew he lied. Hell, he'd probably started falling in love the moment he'd looked into

Edward's dark eyes. He didn't know if it was the right time to say anything about that or not. Yet Scott was right. When the band went back on tour, he'd have to decide how much work he wanted to put into what he had with Edward. That was…if Edward wanted their relationship to continue.

"Well, hello there."

Turning at the sound of the voice, Hunter saw Scout standing in the doorway. Somehow, he hadn't actually been introduced to the man, even in the time he'd been on the farm. Edward had said Scout had headed out to some shows in the area after getting Edward settled back home.

"I'm gone for a week and Edward is overrun by gorgeous men." Scout blinked when he spotted Hunter. "Wait. You look familiar."

"I was in the café when you stopped there to pick up an order last week," Hunter reminded him. "But we weren't formally introduced. I'm Hunter Lee."

"Scout Cavanaugh. Nice to meet you. How exactly did you end up here?" Scout waved his hand vaguely.

Hunter chuckled. "It's a long story, but I met Edward in the park and one thing led to another. Now I'm staying with him before my band heads out on tour."

Scout's pale blond eyebrows shot up in surprise. "Staying with him?" Scout pursed his lips. "I always miss the good stuff."

"He asked me to stay with him and the rest of the band is staying in one of the cottages. Andey Mahan, Scott Clark, Lonnie Balet and Boris McKenzie. This is another of Edward's riders. Are you also a trainer?" Hunter introduced the rest of the guys, noticing how Scout's hand and gaze lingered on Andey.

"An-day? That's an intriguing name," Scout murmured.

"Andey with an E. Makes me unique." Andey shrugged. "Just a little different from the usual Andys in the world."

Scout nodded then turned to answer Hunter. "Not yet. Still moving up the ranks. Another year or two and I'll have people asking me for advice and clients wanting me to work with their horses." Scout definitely didn't lack from a shortage of confidence.

Andey stared at Scout as though he were a Marleaux bass guitar — and Andey coveted one of those above all others. Hunter motioned with his head to Scott, Boris and Lonnie, and they eased away from those two. *Give them a chance to flirt without us watching. Not that it ever bothered Andey, and I'm pretty sure Scout would flirt with anyone he's attracted to.*

"How much you want to bet Andey ends up in that man's bed tonight?" Lonnie wiggled his eyebrows at Hunter.

"I wouldn't take that bet. It's a sure thing," Edward said as he walked in. "Scout, stop flirting with the man and get out in the arena. I want you to take Salt over the liverpool a few times. You need to be able to sense when your mount is going to duck out on you and Salt's been acting up today."

"Yes, sir." Scout said something to Andey that made him blush then strolled out. "Are you coming?"

Edward nodded. "I'll be out in a minute. Thought I'd come in and save these men from your dubious charms."

They all laughed when Scout flipped Edward off. Hunter didn't even hesitate as he stepped forward and brushed a kiss over Edward's mouth.

"Looks like you've been having a good day," he said when he eased back.

"It got even better," Edward replied. "I'm glad to see your friends made it safe. Remember we're having dinner at six tonight, so don't get too caught up in your music."

Hunter smiled. "Don't get too caught up in your horses that you forget."

He watched as Edward walked back out then turned to see all of his friends staring at him. "Why are you standing there, grinning like idiots?"

"Someone's got it bad," Lonnie said in a singsong voice.

"I can't wait until you all fall in love, so I can tease you mercilessly. Well, all except Scott, since it seems as though he's already fallen in love without any of us knowing." Hunter winked at Scott and his friend shrugged. "Can we not discuss my love life and get back to the cottage? I'd like to practice *Blue Baby* one more time today."

"Good plan." Boris led the charge out of the barn and back to the garage.

Hunter trailed behind, happy that all his friends were there and they were doing what they loved. For the first time, he was actually at peace in an odd way, as though he'd found his home base. While touring, he'd always had the strangest sense of being unanchored, even with the guys around. Yet here at Edward's farm, it felt like home, and he wasn't sure he was ready to give that feeling up.

Chapter Nineteen

Edward jumped to his feet when Derek's car drive up to the house. He'd been waiting impatiently on the porch since he'd gotten Max's call that they were almost there. They had talked almost every day, though it'd been a month since they'd seen each other right after Edward's injury.

Yet so much had happened and Edward couldn't wait for his brother to meet Hunter. He wanted them to like each other because he was pretty sure he loved Hunter. It would be a shock to Derek. Edward hadn't mentioned anything about feeling that way during their calls.

Of course, he hadn't realized how he felt until he'd talked to Juan about Hunter one night.

"For the first time in a long time…" Edward paused for a second then continued, *"Probably since Samantha got sick, I'm not looking forward to leaving for the shows. I mean, I want to ride and compete, but I feel like I'm leaving something more important behind."*

Juan shot him a knowing look. "You are leaving someone more important behind. You just haven't figured it out yet."

"What are you talking about?" He glowered at his friend.

"How do you think I feel every time I have to leave Yancey? And why after my classes are done, I'm in a hurry to get back here?" Juan leaned forward, resting his hand on Edward's arm. "You're in love, my friend, and it's marvelous to see."

His first instinct was to deny it, but then he thought about how he'd been feeling the past week, ever since he'd met Hunter. Usually he was overstressed with decisions for the benefit, the upcoming shows, his horses and his clients. Yet every night when he left the barn, all those issues and problems stayed there.

He'd step into his house and smell whatever Hunter had made them for dinner. The dogs would rush to greet him, then Hunter would give him a kiss to welcome him home. That was the thing. Hunter being in his house and his life made the farm feel like home in a way no one had ever done before.

"There you go. Now you've figured it out," Juan informed him.

"How can you be so sure? We've only known each other for a week. I don't believe in love at first sight."

Juan looked up at the ceiling then back at Edward. "Of course you don't. But here's the thing. You don't have to believe for it to happen. It's not like you get struck by lightning either. Sometimes love at first sight can be just as simple as looking into someone's eyes and seeing a part of you that's been missing since you were born."

Edward stared at Juan. "When did you become so wise?"

Shrugging, Juan stood. "When I fell in love with a man who makes my world a better place. Now I'm going home to said man. I'll see you in the morning."

Juan had left and Edward had sat in his darkened office, thinking about their conversation until Hunter had texted him and asked if he was coming home for dinner. Just that simple question and the way his heart had leaped when he'd read it told Edward all he needed to know. He had to figure out a way to tell Hunter how he felt.

"Hey there, big brother. You're looking a lot better than the last time I saw you," Derek said as he climbed out of the car.

Edward threw his arms around Derek, remembering at the last minute to be careful with his cast. "I'm feeling better too," he replied.

They hugged for a moment, then Derek stepped back to let Max embrace Edward.

"Max, great to see you too."

Once their greetings were done, Edward asked, "Did you want to go inside and relax? Or wander around the farm?"

Max cleared his throat. "You know I want to check out the horses, Edward, but whatever Derek wants works for me.

It's not like I won't have time to do it since we're in town for a week."

Edward looked at Derek. "Well?"

"After the flight then the drive, I need to stretch my legs. I want to see how the new additions are growing." Derek took Max's hand then motioned for Edward to go ahead of them. "How's Gypsy doing?"

"He's hanging in there. I'll probably cut the amount of mares he covers next season in half. I've bought back two of his sons and they're both being retired in the next month so I can continue his bloodlines without working him too much." Edward sighed. "It's hard watching him grow old."

"Aye, it is, mate, but he still has a few good years left in him and you'll treat him like the king he is." Max clapped him on the shoulder, his Aussie accent shining through.

As they got close to the paddock where he kept the three rescue cows, Derek stopped and tipped his head. "Where's the music coming from?"

Edward pointed at the Blue Cottage. "Hunter's band is practicing in the garage. I sent you their CD, remember?"

"Right, and you said you hired them to open for me." Derek wandered in that direction.

"You do know we're going to lose him, right?" Max questioned as they trailed in his wake.

Edward smirked. "I would've been shocked if we didn't. The one thing Derek can't resist—aside from you—is good music. This band is one of the best I've heard in a long time."

Max squinted at him. "You're not just saying it because your boyfriend plays in it?"

"No. You know better than that, Max." Edward stopped in the open doorway and smiled at the stunned looks on the band members' faces as Derek greeted them. "I told you he was arriving today," he reminded them.

Hunter stuck out his tongue at him. "Yeah, you did, but knowing and seeing him are two different things."

Derek gestured for Edward to shut up. "I really liked that song you were playing. Did one of you write it?"

Lonnie used his microphone to point at Hunter. "He did, but he doesn't think it's good enough for us to play in our concerts. We've been trying to tell him he's an idiot."

Hunter rolled his eyes and Andey groaned.

"As always, asshole, you're the soul of tact," Boris muttered.

"Don't worry, man. I've felt the same way about a lot of songs I've written that have gone on to be number one hits. I think every writer doubts the brilliance of his words from time to time." Derek patted Hunter on the shoulder. "Can I join you? I'd love to hear the song from the beginning. Maybe convince you to let me sing it on my next album."

The shocked expression on Hunter's face caused Edward and Max to double over laughing.

"Shut up, jerks," Hunter ordered then looked horrified when he realized he might have just insulted Derek St. Martin's husband.

"Oh, they are. Go drool over the horses, you two. When you're done, come on back." Derek shooed them out. "And, Max love, we're not buying any of Edward's horses, remember?"

Max chuckled. "Right. None of Edward's."

As they got out of earshot, Max glanced at him. "He didn't say I couldn't buy any of the animals that you don't own."

"One of the charities I donate to just dropped off a beautiful little Standardbred filly. I think she could be trained into a good cow pony. Just needs a gentle hand right now," Edward told Max. "I'll give you first shot at her because I'm pretty sure when Randy or Tammy see her, they'll fight over her."

"You know Derek's going to kill you when he finds out I bought another horse," Max commented as they meandered to the quarantine barn, where all the new horses stayed until cleared by a vet.

Edward shot Max an incredulous look. "Seriously? My brother thinks you hung the moon, Max. He's not going to get angry with you about a horse. It's just like him buying another guitar. Hell, some of the instruments he buys are more expensive than your horses."

"True. Let's go shopping."

As they entered the barn, Edward thought about how happy he was to have his family there, and how family now included Hunter.

* * * *

"You all ready for this?" Derek asked the band as they stood just off the stage.

The benefit had been a huge success so far. The silent and live auctions had raised thousands of dollars for the charities while giving them some much-needed media attention. Edward had introduced Hunter to so many of Edward's associates and friends he didn't know how Hunter was going to keep all of their names straight.

Now it was time for them to perform. He looked at the five band members and smiled. There were nerves in the way they shifted from one foot to the other. Boris kept drumming his fingers on his leg as though he were playing his keyboard. Edward wanted to tell them the good news, but he'd promised Derek not to say anything. It was Derek's job to explain to the band afterward.

"Yes, we are. It's not like we haven't done this a thousand times before." Lonnie was the only one who didn't look nervous.

"Well, excuse me, Mr. Old Timer. Get your asses on stage and play like you're at Madison Square Garden," Derek ordered them.

While they were taking their places, Edward went out to introduce them. "The band that's going to play for you now is amazing. I'm being honest here, even though you all might think I'm a little biased since the man I love plays lead guitar. Here's Merging Violently."

The stunned expression on Hunter's face and the tears in the man's eyes told Edward all he needed to know. Maybe he should've chosen a more private venue to tell Hunter how he felt, but he wanted the whole world to know and this was the best way to announce it.

"We'll talk later," he mouthed as he walked off stage.

Hunter nodded then the band launched into their first song. Derek grabbed Edward in a hard hug.

"I can't believe you finally fell in love, Eddie. After all these years, and to a man who's going to be as famous as you are someday." Derek squeezed him tight then let him go. "I'll get to be best man at your wedding, right?"

Max hugged him as well, along with Les, Randy and all the other men and women who had become his family over the years.

"Planning a wedding might be jumping the gun, Derek. I haven't even told him face-to-face yet. Plus we're still going to have to deal with both of us being on the road more months than not."

The one worry he had was that their relationship wouldn't last the rigors of their careers. Hunter's was about to take off in ways he'd never imagined and Edward hoped they'd built a strong enough base on which to grow.

Les dismissed Edward's worries. "I've seen the two of you together. You don't have to worry about that. It's a lot easier nowadays to stay in touch, plus if you ever want to go visit him, just give me a call and you can borrow my plane."

"Or mine," Derek offered. "Sure, it'll take work, but like someone once said, 'anything worth having takes effort'."

He took those words to heart while listening to the band's set. Once they were finished, he went back out to introduce Derek. After his brother had taken the stage, Edward took a hold of Hunter and dragged him off into the shadows.

"What the fuck was that? You don't just announce you love me to hundreds of people when I can't do anything about it," Hunter complained then threw himself into Edward's arms.

Their kiss was hard and passionate, but filled with so

much love. If they didn't have to stay for another hour or so, Edward would've taken Hunter back to their house to show him how deeply he loved him.

"I love you too, in case you were wondering," Hunter told him when they stood panting after the kiss. "I was trying to figure out how to tell you."

"Derek's going to ask you and the guys to be his opening act on his new tour," Edward blurted then slapped his hand over his mouth. "Fuck! I wasn't supposed to tell you that. Derek wanted to talk to you about it himself."

Hunter stared at him. "Seriously? Opening act for a Derek St. Martin tour?"

Edward winced. "Yes…and I think there might have been something said about signing you to a record deal."

"Holy shit!" Hunter started to dance in place, but a thought must have struck him because he froze. "Wait a minute. He's not doing this because you love me, is he? It's not like a handout to his brother's boyfriend?"

"Trust me. Derek would never do something like that. He has more respect for me than that and he's not going to risk the reputation of his label on signing a band he doesn't like himself." Edward cupped Hunter's face in his hands. "No, my love. You got this all on your own. Well, you and the rest of the band."

Hunter's face flushed with excitement. "But how are we going to do this? You're going to be traveling to horse shows and I'll be touring. We won't have a lot of time together in the same place."

"Then we make time, Hunter. I'm determined to make this work, even if we have to throw a dart and pick a city to meet in, and borrow our friends' planes. Also, if you decide to sign with Derek, you'll be down in Austin at his ranch, cutting a new album for a couple months. I can come and visit you there." Edward rubbed his thumb over Hunter's bottom lip. "It's all about making an effort and I, for one, am more than willing to do so."

Hunter covered Edward's hands with his then lowered

them to press against his chest. "I was thinking the other day that this farm of yours feels like home and I never want to leave it. You're my family now, Edward. We might come from two different worlds—music and horses—but we can merge them into something beautiful as long as we're together."

"We'll be together forever, if I have my way." Edward bent to seal his promise with a kiss.

He had a feeling the next twenty years of his life were going to be a wild ride, but he'd gone on some crazy ones before. As long as they hung on to each other, they'd come out of the craziness just fine.

No Going Home

Excerpt

Chapter One

"Damn horse," Randy Hersch muttered as he shifted, trying to find a comfortable spot in the seat of his truck. His body ached, he wanted to stop and rest for a while. He'd spent the last two weeks in hospital, and he had a sudden urge to go back to the Rocking H and see his family. He hadn't called to let his sister know he was injured or that he was coming home.

He stopped the truck at the beginning of the driveway and stared at the buildings. The Rocky Mountains proved a beautiful background for the ranch he'd grown up on and had left when he was eighteen. The anger and hate between him and his father had got to the point that he had known one of them would end up killing the other if he had stayed. Randy had left the day after graduation and hardly came back anymore. After getting his leg broken and his body stomped on by an angry bronc, he'd decided it was time for a visit.

It had been a year since he'd last been home. The ranch didn't look like it used to. No longer were the barns painted the dull grey his father seemed to favour. They were the bright blue he'd come to associate with clear Wyoming skies. The windows and doors were trimmed in pristine white. There were three more new buildings on the other side of the main house — he remembered his sister telling him they'd had to build more foaling barns.

It's not home anymore, he thought as he drove up to the main barn, which was filled with organised chaos. His sister Tammy stood in the aisle, directing the ranch hands. He climbed stiffly out of his truck.

"Hey, sis, what's the circus for?" He made his way to her.

Tammy whipped around. Squealing, she raced towards him. He was only able to stop her from launching herself at him at the last moment.

"Wait, girl. Be careful. I'm bruised." He accepted a gentle hug from his favourite sibling.

"Oh, Randy, are you here to recuperate or to stay?" Her gaze traced over his body.

"Staying's never been an option for me, Tammy. You know how Dad feels about me." He shoved his hat back on his head. She wrinkled her nose but kept quiet as he took in the view of spindly-legged foals gambolling beside their mothers.

"What are you doing with the babies?"

Her face lit up. "It's time to pay the rent on those three hundred acres Daddy leased from our neighbour, Les Hardin."

"What does the rent have to do with the foals?" He scratched the velvety nose of one of the mares.

"Les gets his pick of each year's foals. That's what we pay."

"Wait a minute. Who set up that deal? He's robbing you." Randy was furious.

The Rocking H bred and trained some of the country's best cutting horses. Each one of the foals was worth tens of thousands of dollars and it was far more than the property they were leasing was worth.

"Wait, Randy. Don't go off half-cocked. Les and I worked out a deal. Just wait and watch." She pointed to the plume of dust heading towards them. "He's here."

Randy bit his lip and fought back the urge to argue. He wasn't going to treat his sister the way their father treated him. Tammy had taken over running much of the ranch when she'd turned eighteen. He had to trust that she knew what she was doing.

He stood back as a beat-up black truck clattered into the yard. When the tall man wearing a black cowboy hat stepped from the vehicle, Randy clenched his fist and pressed it to his stomach. He'd never felt such a kick of attraction before in his life.

Les Hardin was an inch or two taller than Randy was. His hair was cut short enough to be covered by the cowboy hat. The tanned skin attested to hours in the sun. Les' thin lips pulled up in a smile as Tammy greeted him, but Randy got a look at the man's eyes when he tilted his hat back. Dark brown, and filled with a sorrow so deep Randy was sure he'd drown in it. Here was a man who has lost everything important to him, Randy thought.

Randy's dick hardened and he groaned. He didn't want to lust after this man. He didn't want to get involved with anyone near the ranch. Avoiding any possibility of that made his life more peaceful when he did come back. At least, it was one less reason for his father to hassle him.

Those brown eyes turned his way and he realised Tammy was waving for him to come over. Reluctance dogged his steps. Why did he get the feeling this man would change his life?

"Les, this is my older brother Randy," Tammy introduced them.

"Ah, the bronc rider."

Les' voice was a deep honey drawl. Randy's skin tingled where the man's eyes studied the cuts on his face.

"Did you stick?"

Blinking, Randy realised Les was talking to him. "Yeah, made eight. Then the pickup rider screwed up. Dropped my ass right in front of the bitch and she stomped the shit out of me." He held out his hand. "You must be Les Hardin. Heard you bought Old Jake's place."

He fought back the shiver threatening to race down his spine when Les' rough, calloused hand closed around his and shook.

"Yes, I did. It was bigger than I was looking for, but it was available when I needed it."

Something flickered in those sad eyes, but it was gone before he could make it out.

"Good thing we were looking for land to lease." Tammy grabbed Les' arm and dragged him towards the mares and their babies.

Disappointment burned in Randy's stomach. First man in a while he'd been seriously attracted to and it looked like his sister had prior claim. Didn't it figure that some of the best-looking ones weren't gay?

He made his way to where Tammy was gushing over the babies. He stood close enough to listen in on their conversation but not close enough to put a damper on it.

"Tammy, Jackson said to meet him out at the usual place tonight if you're interested." Les' voice was low, as if he didn't want anyone else to hear.

"Oh, he's back from Arizona? How'd the show go down there?"

"We added a few more ribbons to the Black Bart legion. You'll be getting a few calls, I'm sure."

Randy smiled. Black Bart was the Rocking H's top stud. He'd bet half of the year's crop was Bart's offspring.

"Great. I'll get the scoop from Jackson later." She winked at Les and said, "See any you like?"

"They're all beautiful, Tammy, but where's the one you

really want to show me?" Les' drawl had become brisk.

Tammy's face dropped. "Sorry. I'll show him to you."

Randy started to step forward. He had vowed to stay out of it, but no one was going to talk to his sister that way.

More books from
T.A. Chase

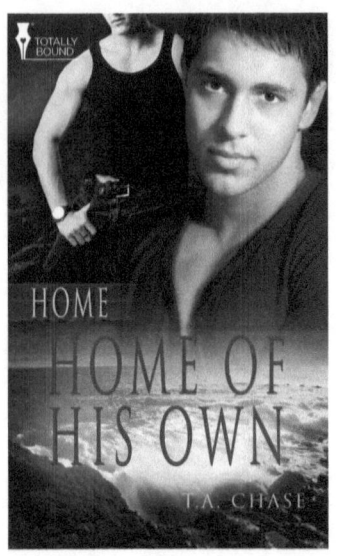

Tony Romanos is a bull rider searching for a place to call his own, and a man to love him no matter what.

Finding a solution for his boss brings Ion to the point of having his deepest fantasies come true.

*Surrounded by secrets, two men search for a serial killer,
while trying to keep it from becoming personal.*

For Pestilence, the White Horseman, love becomes the most powerful cure.

About the Author

T.A. Chase

There is beauty in every kind of love, so why not live a life without boundaries? Experiencing everything the world offers fascinates TA and writing about the things that make each of us unique is how she shares those insights. When not writing, TA's watching movies, reading and living life to the fullest.

T.A. Chase loves to hear from readers. You can find contact information, website details and an author profile page at https://www.pride-publishing.com/